My guide to surviving the zombie apocalypse: day one till day seven

By ross chandler (aka reaper)

My name is Ross chandler and I am from a small town called Knaresborough where most of the events that follow happened this is how I survived the zombie apocalypse through all the terrors and accounts of all the people I have met and those who didn't make it to read this

Day one: infections rising

My day started the same as it always had wake up have a coffee quickly check the news feeds and then head into work. I remember hearing about a cotangent virus that was spreading but it was in Europe and so their was nothing to worry about I thought how I wish I had listened closer and that it was spreading like wild fire. I worked in a care home with people who where very sick and so to me it came as no surprise when a few of the residents had been taken to hospital with sickness.

As I walked into work after the twenty minute walk into work I was met by one of my friends and coworkers called remi. Me and him always had a laugh when working together never taking anything to serious. The nurses where in the briefing room giving out hand over to the staff and requesting if anyone we where caring for had any sickness to straight away report it to the head nurse on the unit as one of the other units was under quarantine for a nasty bug causing sickness and diorama. Their was five staff on me remi ibz Tracy and an agency. It was 7:20 a.m. by the time hand over was fully given and we set out to care for all the residents.

I had been paired up with Tracy to work with for the day. She was such a lovely carer and had a heart of only good intentions. We started our rounds when suddenly the house manager burst in and requested all staff to come to the lounge with urgency. And so all staff came in and the news was switched on to bbc news at 8:00 a.m. it was pictures of London on fire from a helicopter when the camera zoomed in we could see riots in the streets people attacking people and the news reader reported that this was happening not just in Europe but in fact all over the world at the same time and that new York France all other countries had no communications coming out of them and that the army was on standby. The manager looked up at us and asked if anyone had family in London and that if they did they could use their phones to try contact them if not that they could try to get home and try to contact other relatives. me and Tracy went back to work as we where local and had a full house of residents to care for so everyone went back to work except the agency who's family was from London he left to go try find his family little did he no he was driving into chaos and hell on earth .

Cleaning up after finishing helping a resident out of the shower I hear helicopters flying overhead but around knaresborough this always happens as we live so close to an army base its bound to happen but still sends shivers down my spine as I think about what we saw earlier on the telly "ross are you with us or them up their" Tracy laughs I snap back to reality and return to helping hoist the resident back onto his bed and help her dry him off as soon as he is dried we call for a nurse to come do his dressings however when we hit the call bell there is no answer. I decide to investigate when I get to the nurses station I see the room is empty so I think id have a look in some of the rooms to check in if they are in their not till the last room do I see a nurse getting into the back of an ambulance while the other hands over documents of a resident who had fallen sick with symptoms of the virus so I waited for her to return to the unit as all careers where asked to remain on the unit that they worked on to stop the spread it was still early in the morning however the day in day out tasks had been done. I was asked to go on my break and so I took it on the unit pulled my phone out and checked the news all it said was will be updated shortly when new news was realized waiting for the government to put into effect or something that's when I saw the army driving past and again it is not unseen in the area I just assumed they were heading south to help the situation down south when they stopped and put up a road blockade towards the motorway I started to get very worried.

Lunchtime couldn't come quick enough I assisted a resident to have their meal support today was fish Friday and so it was fish and chips or jacket potato for lunch with a choice of soup or salad to start with once he had had his food off he went and left the dinning room for the staff to eat. It was commonly known by residents and staff that staff would eat after. Had any management cottoned on they would never have let us eat it or they would have charged us so a deal was made between staff and residents. So I grabbed my fish and chips and went down to sit near the t.v we had kept it on news all morning for any further updates however now only bbc north Yorkshire was active as the south had gone dark all my colleges came in and got their food as well as the nurses remi came in and started joking about how shit his morning had been and that he couldn't wait to get home to his wife and kids we all looked at him Asif to say you love it hear to much. Many times he had threatened to quit but never pulled through with it always empty threats we al laugh at him and I make him another coffee as that is what us careers live on just encase there is ever a time when this kind of stuff becomes useful again when all of a sudden on the t.v the news presenter was thrown to one side by a man who rugby tackled him when he rose he had blood all over his face and could hear the screams from the studio it was only thirty miles away from where we all sat joking and laughing thinking this was some kind of joke when it finally hit us this has been spreading across the country while we have all been hear at work I looked out at the army blockade hoping and preying that it was all clear when I noticed running across the fields was what could only be described as a horde of people they where heading straight for us the army pulled in front of them and started firing at them but they just kept pushing forwards the guns where so loud I ran along side all the staff some heading for the car park to try get to their cars and others to lock ourselves in the unit closing all the heavy doors to try prolong them getting in I was in shock I had no idea what to do after spending so long playing zombie games its completely different than real life but I hated to call them zombies I headed to the nurses station Tracy came with me and so did remi I locked down the unit hitting the fire button. After such a short time the gunfire stopped and the screaming was all that was left then silence the head nurse came to the office asking what the hell I was playing at hitting the alarm and that the whole home was locked down I dragged her into the office and looked down the corridor it then dawned on me that one resident liked to go outside I ran down the corridor to find the door wide open he was outside being chased by one of them things I wish I could say I tried to save him I closed the door and turned the lock as they where already on him biting him his calls and cries chill me even to this day when I got back to the office most of the residents rooms had windows smashed and people crawling in biting and eating them I locked all the doors even though it hurt me to do it survival had kicked in the people on our unit where very very sick and so I was saving the fit and healthy any that could get out of their rooms by them selves I dragged out and into the corridor and secured it I hear the smashing of windows and doors from the other units I looked at my phone I still had signal so I called my brother and my mum they where at home I told them to lock the doors draw the blinds and hide in the cellar I would try to figure out a way to get home at a later point I guessed that their was enough food in the house for about a week I snapped back to the room and realized what was happening I was so afraid and felt so alone even though I had remi Tracy and the nurses I felt so sad that we had lost so many so fast I fell to my knees and started crying

2:30 p.m

I realized it was going to get dark soon and then it would be impossible to make it to family and friends I thought maybe there was a chance that this could all just be a big joke that the whole of Knaresborough was aware of that I wasn't I looked up and realized that the roof had an access panel in the nurses station I could see and nearly reach I asked remi to give me a push up as there is a ladder on the roof when I started with the company they showed us the emergency exit so that if there was ever a need for it that we could use it to get out however I didn't know where it came down or if any of them things where still out their when I got up I could see smoke coming from Knaresborough and could hear in the distance gunfire and plans dropping bombs on the town I laid down and crawled my way to the edge of the building and what I saw made me nearly throw up their was so many bodies all over the car park some were raising up somewhere being eaten and some the heads gone it was like a horror film in front of me when remi joined me he was sick we needed to figure out a way to distract them to get out safely and get back to our families I called mum again no answer this time I tried nick same then the network went dead "shit not now" I said I didn't even want to think about the worst case scenario remi was with the army for a few years so he took charge and said ok if you can distract them I can go get that APC (armored personal carrier) I asked what he wanted me to do he said run as fast as you can hope they can't catch you I'll get that APC and bring it round front get staff in it then get the fuck out of here he grabbed a metal pole handed it to me and said if they get close smash them don't think about them as people I had so much respect for remi and never asked him what he did with the army as he was closed about that but now was not the time to ask he pointed me to the stairs said run around the walk that has just been finished draw them to you and run the course that should be enough time for me to get it working again and get everyone in it I slipped back down to the nurses station asked the nurse to get all the medicine she could carry in bags and be ready for remi signal and that it will have to be fast and head back up head for the ladder down to the outside when I first got down the ladder I thought maybe I could just sneak away and they wouldn't notice me how wrong I was their was a few of them close and noticed me as I descended so I jumped started shouting drawing their attention to me as I was running around more and more came into view I was so scared but kept on moving as I couldn't stop otherwise id die and become one of them one came close to me so I did what remi said and smashed it I heard its skull smash I had been running for what felt like a whole day when I ran into the open and saw the infected running straight at me I froze this is where remi told me to run to where the fuck was he maybe he slipped out and did what I was thinking about doing then all of a sudden their was loud bangs all round me I realized it was gun fire I looked over my shoulder remi on top of the APC with the 0.50 cal shooting at them killing them and putting them down so fast then he motioned at me to get into the APC he came down into locked the hatch I saw the nurse shaking and my colleges looking at remi as if he was a god that saved their lives I had applied to the army but been declined on medical grounds however I had been to the rifle range so when he handed me a ball point .22 and asked if I new my way round it I removed the clip checked the iron sight and reloaded it they where all very nervous about this Tracy finally spoke up and asked "what the fuck are we going to do now we cant live in this tin can" I remembered my home is literally down the road two minutes in this thing I lived in a quad with one way in three ways out I suggested that we went their it is like a fort and their will be food as all the nabours had gone away to Spain and left their keys to us to look after all of the staff wanted to go to their families remi suggested that we drive to each me and him would take point (I had no idea what all this meant) since I was closest to the home when me and remi entered the yard I could see my back door was open he looked at me as if to say do you want me to go first I shook my head I entered the house and we slowly progressed into the house I firstly went upstairs all the blinds where closed as I had ordered I was working my way up as I had camouflage gear and a backpack military grade remi looked impressed when I walked out with two of them combat knives and a few swords offered him them and my bow he took a combat knife but left the bow for me we moved into my mums room it was empty thank god I thought but then worry came over me where was she and where was nick his bow was missing and so was his car keys but his car was outside so where the fuck where they I then remembered I told them to hide in the basement I went to the door it looked like it had been recently opened remi tapped his hand on my shoulder (again didn't no military did this) as I opened the door nick appeared with his bow drawn and mum behind him with a knife he shouted I grabbed his mouth and told him to shut the fuck up he looked so scared to be honest we all where I signaled them to come out to the APC quietly we moved slowly when we where all outside in the yard I realized that it was getting late I told them to lock the door behind me and that id be back soon with others nick nodded I left him in charge of the yard fortifications he asked if their was any chance we could grab food as we went I looked at him like seriously

5:00 p.m

Back in the APC travelling to staffs houses getting food and clothes trying desperately to find family of them ibzs house was next when we entered he had a sword drawn he called quietly to his wife but the door was wide open and a blood trail had been scene out the front door aiming inwards so me and remi moved forwards all of a sudden his wife appeared with a bite mark on her hand but she hadn't turned confused ibz went to his wife embraced her and asked where his son was she cried and pointed upstairs he ran up and what followed will haunt me till the day I die at least I had no children what we saw was his seven year old son dead on the floor his head separated from his body he wanted to bury the body in the garden however their wasn't time his wife leapt on his back and started to bite down into his neck his screams could be heard for miles and miles gushes of blood came squirting out of his neck he fell to the ground to which remi pulled out his mp5 and shot her in the chest she kept coming so I he shot again this time aiming for the head she went down all of a sudden over the fence five or six more came over he carefully aimed and hit his target while I covered our exit I could see more coming down the street I told him to run we didn't have time to stay and burry our fallen ibz started to twitch so I aimed my .22 at him shot and drew the cross as we left I'm sorry brother in another time another universe id of stayed side by side we got back to the APC Tracy's husband had driven them before in the T.A as soon as we got to it he was driving so we had a rolling start remi got straight on the .50 cal and started firing at the oncoming horde I then remembered how where we going to park this death machine and have everyone get out and into the safety of the yard that's when I figured it out if we parked it with the back door to gate it could be a quick get away in an emergency the drive back to mine was only ten minutes but it felt like forever when we arrived I told nick to open the gate only enough for us to back up onto it we then unloaded the APC with all the food weapons and fuel and the door of the APC was perfect fit for the gate giving us a quick get away I got everyone into the houses around us told them to stay quiet while we figured out our next step fighter plans where still flying over meaning their was still people fighting the zombies remi grabbed the walkie talkies from the APC long range ones and sat out on the wall listening to see if anyone was communicating about what was going on he came down shortly after and was checking stock on weapons and foods he pulled me to one side and said to me that I needed to be able to learn how to fire other guns I was exhausted needed to rest he excepted this but said if we are to survive we needed everyone to help out he then went back onto the wall it was a high wall so he could see the streets I decided id try make a dash for the shops that where close by I told him this he said he'd rather have two go than one however I said I no these streets I no the shops I new everything about the layout of the whole town so he agreed but I had to get into black clothing all the electric had gone off by this point so it would mean id be moving in the darkness I remembered the quietest way to Tesco the closest shop to me I figured id try their the doors where wide open no looters had been hear yet I'm guessing as it all happened so dam fast before I left the nurse asked me to pop into the pharmacy next door and get whatever I could but I prioritized the food with three military backpacks on two with food and water with cigarettes then went next door to the pharmacy grabbed everything that I could carry at that exact moment a zombie crashed into the store I had left my weapon back at the house I only had my knife I no one bite and I become one how quick is unknown yet that's when the impossible happened I saw Scott the zombie must of followed him in and was locked onto him so it might not notice me so I could sneak up and either kill it or escape I decided that killing it and sparing him would be the best more humans to fight the dead in my mind I slide up behind it and stabbed it in the head it dropped I grabbed it to soften the fall to make sure nothing else heard the noise Scott noticed me and the knife he panicked as I was wherein a face mask I pulled it down he smiled I asked if Sarah and josh where alive and where were they hiding he said that he saw me leaving Tesco so he'd follow me and that they where in the car down the ally way I walked back with him quietly to his car Sarah smiled when she saw me then she saw the knife and looked nervous I held it back so she wouldn't be jumpy placed it on the ground and walked forward josh looked weak and she looked scared I asked Scott how josh was feeling he is under the weather I told them we had a nurse and a solider with us at my house Sarah looked like she could cry I asked if they wanted to come join up with us and that we had room and that the car might be useful at that very second another zombie appeared it was scot that pulled out a knife and ran at it. it nocked him over within seconds I was upon it I dragged it off when I realized it was an old friend from school I stabbed it in the side of the head but not before it let out a howl and called in more of its brothers I grabbed Scott and he jumped in the car I told him drive around for a while they will disperse we can go back for more later he agreed I wanted to get Sarah and josh safe in the comfort of the house and josh could be looked after we drove quickly to the house parked the car next to the APC giving it extra support I got them into the house they looked drained but I needed to get back out to get gas and other supplies such as sharp weapons for close range attacks Scott got a combat knife told me he was going to come with me I declined as I alone knew the routs and was quietly able to get them to my surprise I get a call to say that a few others had seen the APC and joined up to the group I went and met them it was Gemma my god it was so good to see her see she is my girlfriend I was so happy to see her I gave her the biggest kiss and cuddle she slapped me I looked confused as to why she said that's for not coming for me then she grabbed me and kissed me again I hadn't forgotten her I thought she was in Liverpool she had come home to surprise me I hated myself for not guessing why she was angry with me her mum and dad where with me shit id forgotten her gran lived down the road I ran to the edge my mum called me back and she said Joan is hear too I sighed with relief I jumped up on the wall and asked remi what we should do he advised that we built traps for the zombies and for people who threatened our group I looked at him like are you for real he said it may not be today or tomorrow but eventually it will happen I considered what he had said and suggested I make my way down to the retail park to gather stuff from Argos as I no they stock gas canisters and 02 cylinders he replied only if you take someone with you I ask if I can take Scott then Pete Gemma's dad stepped forward and said no I will go with you we grabbed Scotts car keys and drove quickly down to the retail park it was starting to get really dark now all we could see was zombies walking round and running after a few survivor's I worked down at the Argos a few years earlier and new there is a side entrance that will help us get in and out I could see the shutters to the back where closed but the front doors had been smashed in and the undead where inside not behind the counter we approached the side door it was already open I asked Pete to wait by it and shout if their was any problems I ran up and slid down the ramp god id always wanted to do that when I worked their the back door was open but the shutters where locked luckily I new the managers left the keys inside to open it I found the van keys signaled Pete to come to me opened the back of the van and started loading up the vans with useful materials such as metal gas and sharps I told Pete to drive the car back and id drive the van behind him he agreed as I locked the back door and took the keys I'm not going to lie I haven't driven a van before but iv had a few lessons in cars and guessed it was nearly the same thing we made our way back to the house again parking the car and the van next to the APC giving us a gran vantage point to shoot from if we needed to and unloaded remi was impressed I asked about his family he said he alone would go get them back once he felt we could hold guns without killing ourselves first

11:00 p.m

Remi came off watch and I went onto over watch all the houses where silent it was very aery every now and then a zombie would stumble round the corner as long as it carried on wandering I left it alone as the bullets where limited for now and I didn't want to make to much noise to attract more of them Pete and Scott started making I.E.D (improvised explosive device) under watch of remi I was so worried about how much food we had and so I asked Scott and Pete once they had finished to head back into the town on foot dressed them all up in black gave them knives and a walkie talkie to keep in touch they set off I could see all the fires burning from when the bombs where dropped we got so lucky they didn't drop right on us I thought it might be an idea to paint the roof to make sure if anyone was watching us they could see we where still alive I thought it was a great idea and so did everyone else so I got nick to climb up on the roof to paint the letters on the roof when he climbed down he said it looked the best it could be I asked him to move all the food into the cellar as it was a real worry that we would run out when out of the corner of my eye I saw what I thought was a child it was looking right at me from the shadows I raised my rifle and it moved forward covered in blood it had a bite mark on its neck I felt so sorry for it. it was at that moment that Sarah stepped up next to me she recognized the child it was one of her friends children she started to cry it began running towards the wall I shot it in the head and pulled Sarah in close told her that it was already dead and that it was a zombie she climbed down and went back into the house then Gemma came up and brought me a blanket with a cup of coffee to keep me awake as she handed it to me I heard a scream a woman's scream I looked in the direction it was coming from it was out of sight but I new that scream I new the voice that attached to it. it was samie she was running towards the house I could tell she was getting closer so I signaled to Gemma's to get down and I tried to help her but the zombies where faster than I was she got bit on the leg I shot the zombies as quickly as I could but it was over the second she got bitten I now had the hardest choice to make do I bring her in wounded and infected or do I leave her outside to turn if I bring her in she could turn and kill all of us if I leave her and she's immune she will hold it against me for the rest of my life I decided to go for the first one offer her a hand round to the door that opened at my request I got the nurse to take blood samples and try to help her so she could relax samie looked at me with such gratefulness in her eyes the nurse then asked me if I could possible tomorrow go and grab some equipment to witch I replied it might not be possible without more trained with the guns we shall see what we can do she nodded but asked if we get chance I replied of course we would do what we can at the moment I heard Scott shouting with Pete to get the door open panic in their voices opened quickly as I see in the distance zombies running faster than id ever seen them run I dragged them in remi was one step ahead of me threw i.e.ds out the door and shot them blowing up the mini horde they all where blown away by the explosion more joined the fold I grabbed my rifle and started firing and so did Tracy's husband three against 40 or more zombies as the last one fell remi screamed fuck what the hell happened out their now we have to burn the bodies close to home I looked at him confused he replied if we don't the rats will eat them and get infected we need to burn the bodies to keep the infection out of the area cities will be a no go within a few days maybe weeks he went to the APC grabbed a jerry can with fuel in it pored it over the bodies and then set them on fire I was sick to see the sight and smell of burning flesh it burnt for half an hour I asked if anyone wanted to say a word for the dead no one spoke up so I said ashes to ashes we rise and we fall today the human race has been tested but we have proven we are strong and resilient do not give up otherwise all we have worked so hard for will be for nothing with that everyone went on their way I kept watch just to make sure no more attempted to get in

Day two: life in the dark

I woke in bed thinking and hoping this had all just been a bad dream it was 7:30 as usual I got up got dressed it was due to be my day off had the world not gone to shit before my eyes so I figured id get into plain clothes and head downstairs the hallway was all dark but the sun was starting to rise I tried to turn the light on but it didn't work I thought oh their must have been a power cut or the fuse tripped so I went back into my room hugged Gemma opened my curtains blinds and saw the hell before me and realized it was not just a fucked up dream but in fact was real and that I had been shooting a rifle with remi at other zombies or whatever the fuck they are I can hear so much noise outside I look down and see them all over the place shit this cannot be happening I run downstairs and head out into the yard where everyone is lined up on top of the wall with rifles shotguns and pistols I look at remi who winks at me and says morning sunshine sleep well I retort to him better if you where their winking back when Gemma's dad looked at me I say it was a joke he laughs so does Scott and so does Tracy's husband so I step up in my slippers and pjs grab my rifle remi looks at me and says not today you're going to fire an assault rifle I need you on point with me so he hands me a M14 I look at and then at remi and say you shouldn't have and laugh he replies she's got a kick on her don't think you control her she controls you and I put it into single fire rather than burst I learnt that its better to fire singly than spray it he wasn't wrong it fucking kicked like a mule on speed once I got my Barings with it I looked at remi who was making noise to attract the undead zombie bastards to us to see how we did I missed the first few but after a few practices I got the hang of it once we all became well accustomed to the weapons I look to remi why do you want us to be trained with them so quickly he answered that needed to speak to me privately he spoke to me once inside the house he had received a transmission in the night saying the army was fighting hard but that they had lost the south of the country and where loosing ground not gaining it he wanted to go get his family and wanted to get more equipment from the nearest military base in Harrogate as well as hitting up the hospital for that equipment for the nurse and to look for more survivor's and to gather food and ammunition for the guns being better equipped never hurt anyone he said and so with that I grabbed my cammo gear and he did the same then we emptied our backpacks and gave out more backpacks I asked nick to stay and I asked Pete to stay with his gun he agreed to protect the encampment while we went out and gathered all the necessary's and to keep an eye on samie in case she turned into one of them the horde had dispersed now and was all dead I asked nick to burn them while we were gone

8:30 A.M

All kitted up we jumped into the APC and started to drive off down brigate while remi was on the .50 cal he occasionally fired it when I asked him at a later date he said the reason he fired is if it was to quiet he felt nervous as zombies have been attacking us left right and center we made our way through starbeck nothing much changed their it was always a shithole but its where remi lived we went into his house while we cleared each room we found his children and wife alive so took Andrea and Leo back down to the house left them their to get to no everyone and headed back through starbeck and powered through as we passed the hospital it looked infested when I asked remi about his plan he said he needed better audiences of weapons and explosives that you could only get on a base we where all chatting about what we did in our lives when remi finally opened up about what he did he was with special forces complete black ops outfit he wouldn't fill us in on operations he had been on or where he had been but he told us he would train us to be the best of the best better than standard army it explained a lot about how he knew how to fire all types of guns and his training with knives and survival skills we carry on past the college and up to the army foundation college it had clearly been over run by zombies all the trainees had been torn apart while trying to get to their units or to their homes we made it to the gate that was still closed and so remi was confused as to how they got inside it must have been a solider who was infected turned and took over the base so we must be careful not to get bitten but we don't know how this thing spreads so be careful while we work our way to the armory we slowly progress instead of using loud weapon's we used knives and anything blunt that doesn't make much noise we claw our ways forwards as we reach the mess halls remi suggests we get the food from their like the MRA food that can last years we fill up our backpacks then send Scott and Tracy's husband back with them they empty them bring them back we repeat this process five or six times till we have enough food for a long time we move to the armory as soon as we arrive we get jumped by a man he demands we put down our guns and step outside he doesn't see remi sneak up behind him with his combat knife drawn and presses it to the mans neck who straight away stutters and backs down remi says we don't want to hurt you in fact we can protect you from the monsters outside if you let me get what I need the man agrees remi introduces himself and all of us do the same I look at remi and say maybe the man would feel more comfortable talking without a knife to his neck remi removes the knife and apologizes straight away offers his hand and says what's ur name the man replies my name is Paul I am the armory sergeant remi asks is their anyone else still alive on the base Paul shakes his head remi then picks up clothes and amour tells everyone to do the same picks up a barrot .50 cal its beautiful I say as he hands it to me looking in my eyes and says you think that M14 hurt wait till you feel this all of us grab as much ammo as we can carry and Paul helps us gather grenades and clothing and backpacks we move back to the APC Paul advised us to go to the garage and get another one remi considers this then agrees one for hospital equipment one of army stuff however we remained cautious of this man as he was a stranger remi drove one of the APC and Tracy's husband drove the other Scotts went with remi and I went with Tracy's fella I wanted to try the gun up top I felt like it might prepare me for firing the sniper rifle that remi had just given me how far that was from the truth this gun was mounted and still kicked me hard we where finally ready to depart when suddenly a surj of zombies appeared I fired heavily into the crowd of zombies it tore through them over the radio we hear the signal remi was on about earlier only now it was saying if you where hearing this that the world had lost the war against the zombie virus after two days that it had taken the world by storm and that it is transmitted by bite or blood that the government had fallen and to take refuge where ever you could both our guns now firing at the same time remi threw a grenade into the crowd then screamed get down the ground shook iv never felt such power and presence of death in my entire life now that we had two APC I felt very confident maybe to confident I scream out I am the reaper and I will take your souls a few years before I had a reaper tattoo on my arm so I had finally become the reaper I was over come with pure rage even remi sensed it we started to role off the base seeing less and less zombies and what we couldn't kill we drove over with the APC crushing bones and skulls as we drove it only took two minutes to get to the hospital I asked Scott to stay on over watch on the APC while we went in I grabbed the M14 and Paul also grabbed one remi jumped out of the APC grabbing an A12 Shotgun we went round the back of the hospital as it was the quieter entrance rather than the front where lots of activities we all headed to the labs combat knives drawn when I felt something grab me I see a zombie and then within a flash Paul has stabbed it in the head it slumps I'm so grateful but still very weary of him as we walk into the labs we notice everything is in tact and in the corner of the room is a room sealed off but with shatter proof glass with lots of zombies behind it then notice the people in this room are still alive working on the equipment I cough to get their attention they stop see the body and a woman steps forwards oh dear it appears DR Adam has passed one of them says good riddance that prick tried to assault me yesterday I recognize one of them and realize its Karla she was a nurse on the unit but she was training to do micro biology I asked her if she was safe and if her and her team assuming it was her team at the time wanted to come stay somewhere safe to work as so we didn't have to steal their equipment she agreed when we said the head nurse was with us and working to save someone who was bitten Karla suggested we take all the medicine as well from the hospital try and build up different types of immunity and attempt to kill the virus rather than have to find patient zero I didn't understand a word of what she was saying but having a specialist at this kind of work would be useful we offered to help them pack up their equipment and help protect them while they transported it to the APC which they appreciated however they pointed out that they have been fine up to this point once all the equipment was loaded up we started to move when again I saw a small child in my field of view we now had 6 specialists in with us we had one nurse three two children and six adults two soldiers we had quiet a few in our group now once we reached the yard we backed up the first APC unloaded the food got it into one of the cellars then unloaded the second APC with weapons and tech kit and set them up in another cellar all the houses round our way have cellars as soon as Karla saw samie she wanted to look at the bite but I had to get back outside to figure out what was our next step me and remi and Paul sat and discussed what happened on the base what was their plan and how fast they move in the night I brought up that the children that turned where not like the rest however the others were skeptical except Sarah who had seen the zombie the night before staring at us

12:30

We split up into little raiding parties I needed to no we had fuel and resources to keep the power for the machines up to this point we hadn't needed to have power but now it was crucial to run the machines samie has taken a turn for the worse and the nurse doesn't think she can keep the infection at bay I have gone with Scott down to near where he lives a place called Stockwell there is a company down their that used to sell generators so we thought maybe if we could get a few into the Argos van we might be able to only thing is it's a heavy piece of machinery and the van was running out of fuel so we needed to get some fuel I guess it was a great idea then but at the time we took up a lot of space using jerry cans and I got annoyed as it would take serval journeys to get all the kit we needed I was tired after a long morning and Scott was getting tired too we took a break where I got some energy drinks and some food that was still fresh even after the power had died the freezers where still rather cold we grabbed all the bottles of water that the front cabin could take and headed back down to get the third generator the final one then we could cook food properly and start making progress we had left our weapons back at the yard as it was a retrieval but kept combat knives in our amour and backpacks all of a sudden I saw a familiar face it was ben we went to school together he was all slumped I couldn't tell if he was one of them or not so I drew my weapon regardless he saw us and started to wave If he was a zombie he was an intelligent one at that he walked towards us sadly we didn't notice a zombie came out of the shadows and swiped for him it missed but threw him off his guard and ripped a bit of the flesh he swore and kicked it down to the ground hit it but it bit his hand we were running to his aid but it was to late the zombie got the better of him bit his neck and drained all the life away from him I was close to tears this was one of my closest friends before the event and he had just been killed by this monster I wanted its head on a spike I grabbed my knife out of my bag ran at it Scott followed suit I wanted this piece of shit to suffer for what it had done to my friend I toyed with it willing it to try and turn me it missed every time eventually I stabbed it in its head then went to town stabbing all over its body Scott dragged me off telling me it was over I whipped the blood away from my face and went to bens side he was starting to turn I had to kill one of my close friends that was it I was going to save everyone I promised ben as I smashed his head down on a rock I promised myself id try to save everyone how naïve I was we worked our way back to the house with the body I wanted to burry him properly as soon as remi saw the body grabbed the fuel and tried to burn it I refused to let him I wanted to burry him and so that was what I was going to do as soon as he had been buried samie started to cough up blood she collapsed and started to fit on the floor this was the sign that the virus had won she turned in seconds and tried to bite my ankle but was to slow and I caught her with my knife in the side of the head at one point ben and samie had been a couple so I thought it would be nice to burry them together once this had been done Karla came up from the cellar with some news about the virus even though I was in an extremely bad mood and wanted to kill all zombies she announced that she figured out why it is so aggressive to which I reply I'm aggressive but I'm not contagious she replied noticing my darker side has been revealed don't worry love we can change that soon enough we then all sat down and had our meal except for Scott who stood watch remi finally had time to be with his wife and son who lovingly embraced him Gemma came close to me cuddled me and asked if she could learn to shoot I replied I didn't see why not and that it would be useful if everyone could learn to shoot bar the children I didn't want to put a gun in a child's hand so everyone lined up on the wall and stood waiting for remi he came up to the wall handed out the clips and said use the bullets carefully and sparingly Gemma shot first and hit the target a natural sniper just like your fella looking at me with a gleam in his eyes Gemma says bet I can hit a better shot than ross challenge excepted I retort ok remi says everyone come watch two snipers at war with each other over who can hit the furthest target first one is 100 m away Gemma shoots first hits and then I shoot I miss and Gemma is in a state of disbelief claiming she is the winner and gets to go out to do retrievals and gathering resources out of the building I agree on condition that she takes someone with her at this point nick steps up grabs the rifle points to a target 200 m away hits it dead on and asks if he can do the same I say well fuck it if it takes pressure off me to do the heavy lifting then go for it anyone else want to go out I start to laugh to this day I still have no idea where he came from or how he found me but an old friend of the family Jamie showed up with his wife and daughter and son who is a marine and asks if he can join in on the hard core shooting I jump down off the wall greet him with a hand shake and a hug bring him back inside and ask what he's doing hear and of course we would welcome him at that moment I realized we were getting over populated and might need to re consider where we are living even though it is safe hear there is a lot of us now so I convene with remi Scott Jamie Paul Nick and Tracy the head nurse the medical team we picked up and decided we might be able to construct a better more fortified place close by I sent out scouting parties to different parts of the town and Harrogate as well using the car and the van when they had all returned after something to eat quickly we discussed that Jakub smith field would be a possibility as it has a long rang of site and a high wall that could be fortified only problem would be building a new fortification so we decided to go down to near where Lidl is and grab as much resources as we could carry in the van and car

3:30

We started setting up a wall it wouldn't be finished for days but at least it was a start I mounted the .50 cal at the top of the hill with a massive view of the entire area we planned to populate the APCS could be positioned as century turrets till it was finished but we had a plan the medical team would be the last thing to be moved over as it needed to be protected also the land was fertile so crops could be grown off it if we needed to we set up spikes and then headed back into the town to grab more food and supplies as the work team of Jamie Paul Scott and remi started pooling into the building work making make shift defensive positions and building sheds just to start with by the time it was a small fort it was starting to get dark so we headed back up to the safety of the house I kept sending small parties including Gemma to raid to pharmacy and other shops for clothes and food I decided it might be an idea to go back up to the base in Harrogate so I took Jamie's son and Pete we had M14s we took one of the APCS that Jamie's son rob could drive we filled it with MRAS and more ammo and more military clothing for warmth the head nurse Libby that's her name was doing an inventory on all the medicine being brought back and taken away to make sure nothing got lost or taken by mistake (emphasis on the taken by mistake) while driving back we notice a building that has a sign on the wall saying survivors inside help please we decided to check it out there is a horde of zombies bashing on the door I can see inside there is three men holding the door frame and two woman inside I recognize one of the blokes he was a friend of mine from college Reece he was quite the legend claiming if the zombie apocalypse ever happened he would be ready clearly not but none of us where ready when it hit me rob and Pete take aim and fire clearing the first wave and distracting the second while indicating to get in the back of the APC they nod we drive round killing as many as we can till it looks relatively safe to transfer them into the APC once in we drive them back to Knaresborough to our yard and tell them to wait while we unload the APC turns out we where quiet lucky in finding Reece and his friends as they had all done construction at college one as a brick layer and the other as a plumber Reece was a trained electrician the girls where shop assistants when we found out their skills got them straight to work for us on the new base and sent them with rob to the site of the new location while we dropped the APC back off

9 P.M

Its dark so the team assembling the new fort pull back to the yard pulling the APCS back to a defensive line the parties that had been out looking for resources had found torches and battery's for them was a shame that we had night vision headsets from the army base but the torches could be used in the house as long as they weren't shined on the windows that where being boarded up to stop the zombie hordes being able to get in today has been a difficult day and a hard day but I no there is so much harder to come its going to be no walk in the park but I have a strong feeling we will make it the lads we picked up today their names are john and Dan lads I hadn't met before however I trust Reece to keep them in check he had promised me he would problem was the crowding that was happening so we had to get this done quickly to help sustain ourselves nick was in his element as he had found some cheese from fodder where he worked and he felt like it had been an eternity since he had some cheese I let him enjoy his reward while I help remi clean the weapons then turn them all into Paul as we requested all of the people who where living with us to do out of trust and respect everyone had agreed except for nick as his bow was a personal thing I understood that as long as it was locked away Paul rob and remi had a lot to talk about and discuss I just wanted to cuddle up to Gemma after burring to of my friends that day and not wanting to face what might possibly go wrong the next day or the day after our community was blossoming yet I felt a sense of fear as well as pride me Scott Sarah Gemma josh and Leo sat together and had a meal chatting shit like so many times people joined in as we went joining in finally letting their guard down it was nice even if only for five minutes see this is what makes it all worth it seeing people just being people my mum had been making coffee all day for people but was now making clothes out of old clothes dark ones I decided it might be a good idea to get into one of the houses round the way as a kind of look out for bigger hordes or even people who intend to be harmful towards our group so I made for the house opposite then remembered I live near a church and thought now was as good a time as any to go I remember before the event thinking their cant be a god seeing all the evil in the world now I look at it and think if there is a god then how is he deciding who lives and who dies but I just wanted to go and prey just for a moment upon arrival I saw the carnage that must of happened at the beginning of this chaotic and horrific event of the undead only thing was they where all dead not undead just dead then it dawned upon me people can be just as evil maybe this was the work of someone who is close by not from my camp but what if another group of survivors lived close by and this was meant as a warning or a training ground I went back to the group asked for remi to come with me the second he stepped in he said this is a trap we need to get out of hear now and back to the group before we could get close to the door it slammed shut and dropped us into blackness back to back remi and me went and heard laughter what they didn't realize is we were prepared I dropped to my knees as did remi we lowered our night vision googles and could see where they where and they could see us by being adapted to the dark their leader came forward and spoke I recognized his voice he said if you wish to see the light you must first face the dark I screamed Adam this shit has got to stop look at what has happened hear his response was ohhh you like my work its all for you ross I wanted you to see what iv been doing since you pushed me out of your life and out of Knaresborough remi whispered into my ear do you no this piece of shit Adam replied how can ross not have told you about me we were kins men at one point closer than brothers but he did something to me I can never forgive remi looked at me I said he hurt my sister I retaliated he got hurt bad I made him choose live by leaving Knaresborough or stay and die but this was years ago Adam times have changed Adam replied ohhh I know it has thus why I'm back to finish what we started pulled up my rifle and said lets settle this as men not as cowered in the dark he hadn't realized I could see him he rushes at me with a knife I drop the rifle and pull out my knife and meet him while remi scopes the room out for any possible shooters no one is carrying any guns so he returns to watching the fight Adam swings and hits my arm cutting it rather deep he laughs as if he wants me to beg for my life its not going to happen I retort I didn't want this all these people could have helped in the fight against the undead he smiles who said I want us to win at this point I managed to connect my blade with his leg he slumps onto his side at this point the door slides open the night vision blinds me and remi and Adam the undead are pouring in to the full church I can finally see how many of them there are but the zombies start to tear into the living like an all you can eat buffy Adam rushes to the door claiming that this isn't over as he says that he gets bitten on the neck and hits the deck I pick up the rifle and shoulder it taking the head off the zombie that bit him even though I hate him I still respect him in the aspect that he is a human being as he writhes in agony I with the help of remi start shooting at the undead and the living that helped with this massacre once the room is clear I walk over to Adams undead body and assure him I will see him in hell and in the next life then stab him in the neck and the head he dies I close his eyes and walk away into the night and back to the compound where nick is on edge looking over the wall he sees me walking bleeding from my arms and is opening the gate before I can even explain Libby is trying to cover up my arm to stop anyone thinking I have been bitten I don't want to hide it I want people to no there are people out their who want to hurt us just for the sake of it as well as an act of true hatred she puts stiches in my arm I get some looks but Gemma walks up to me crying hugs me kisses me tells me it will all be ok I ask her what she's on about she asks me if iv seen what's out front I replied no I haven't seen it I look over the wall my sister is lying dead on the ground id assumed she was still in the USA making her way home when this shit storm kicked off nick is crying as am I it's the first time I felt real pain and I new who had caused this shit storm of pain and id been the decent person and made him die a dignified death now I want to get on the ground and pound the lifeless body into the dust but I need to morn rather than hate him I ask remi to go out and retrieve my sisters body so we can burn her in the proper way not leave her out on the road nick had said someone drove past but went to quickly to see who it was god dammit it hurt so much my heart not my arm my arm will heal this will not get better we got her all dressed up nicely and burned her body in the yard on a stack of wood that night many tears where spilt and all because someone wanted revenge for something that happened as children I have to appear strong for the group but everyone knows I'm struggling me and nick share a bottle of whisky to sooth the pain that will never leave us fuck me it hurts everyone huddled up and hugged me and nick I burst away from the group and said enough is enough we need to be looking forward not backwards and that the night will soon be over a new dawn will rise

Day three: old blood old friends

6:30 A.M

I woke with a violent crash and an explosion I got straight into my gear and ran for the wall I saw two helicopter's crash as I arrived I could see fear in remies eyes he looked at me and swore he had intercepted a transmition claiming the last battalion was fighting their way south from Scotland as a resistance to try reclaim lost ground apparently this was the air support for them remi had contacted them on long range frequency (again I didn't realize he knew how to do this) once everyone had assembled in the court yard remi spoke up saying their was a chance the army was still alive or possibly was all lost he asked if anyone would join him to check if their was any survivors and that the rest where to go to work on the new area Paul stepped forwards however remi asked him to stay at Jakub smiths field to keep it safe and secure and so with a bit of encouragement he moved back I said id join remi to see if anyone made it even though everyone was exhausted and my arm still hurt and was bleeding again Libby stepped out and wanted to check it to stop any infection from developing within the wound it was still dark but getting lighter every second and so as the saying goes daylights burning we split into three teams I asked Gemma to stay safe and to

please stay with the others helping pack everything up or going out looking for supplies I hug her close she kisses me I wish I had gone with her as the day would bring so much pain and suffering for the entire group had I realized what was going to happen to me I would of stayed we all say our goodbyes I take nick to one side and tell him to keep watch and to keep a low profile after yesterday I want to keep everyone safe he assures me he will keep over watch on the yard and if anything happened he would call on the radios we set off I was chatting to remi I tell him I want to check a few places to see if anyone else made it we head out towards a village called whixley I saw a few people running from zombies but the APCS where to busy in keeping the field clear so I had to leave them behind all the faces I saw I will never forget all the fallen but these people where trying to just survive when we finally arrived it was a blood bath soldiers wasted all over the floor blood everywhere those that didn't die right away fell prey to the infection and where running around after the villagers killing senselessly as we drove it seemed like hundreds of bodies all over the place I thought about asking to head towards Leeds to get to the armory that I knew of their however remi pointed out that the cities would be the worst place to be with the infection we where discussing it all when suddenly the car we had been in got smashed into by a van all I remember is flipping over then blacking out
....

When I finally came to I could hear the sound of ripping and tearing I look to my left as I realize one of them has got into the car and was eating remi he was starting to turn I felt so much sorrow that he had died and couldn't be left to rest in peace I grab my backpack from the roof as we where upside-down and grabbed the knife from my backpack I grabbed remi and stabbed him in his head a calm came over the recently deceased zombies face I now worked on getting myself out of the car before the other zombie realized that its food wasn't as good as a living person I clawed at the belt the zombie noticed my struggle and started to crawl up to me the flow of remis blood slowed as it showered the zombie I finally hit the buckle and dropped to the floor with a thud I could feel it staring at me looking at me as a meal for it I push the door its jammed so I now realize I have to get out the same way the zombie got it by climbing out of the car on remis side the zombie stood in my way and it could see the way I needed to go but it was locked onto me I hold my knife out and lung I miss its head but hit its neck a spray of blood comes out and just missed my face the zombie tries to bare its teeth down Into my arm as it passes it I pull back quickly knowing one bite is all it takes I re aim and strike it right in the temple smashing the skull and killing the brain it slumps down on the ground I decide to do the decent thing and burn remis body within the car so I climb out of the car look around I see the van that crashed into us the window is smashed and the driver is half out of the window half in the cabin I see that he has turned and is trying to crawl out I no that it was an accident that he crashed into us or at least I hopped it was I get my bearings I am still in whixley so I need to figure out how the hell to get back to Knaresborough I grab my M14 and remis dog tags and his gun I hate to be the one to tell his wife that he has passed I will have to make it seem like he went down fighting rather than dying after being hit by the van I decide to look in the back of the van as soon as I open it I regret it 4 zombies jump out recently turned by the looks of it it stuns me and knocks me over I re gain my balance and stand and run I assumed the driver was trying to get people safe but one of them had been bitten and turned on the rest I decide that ill go on foot its still very early and only a few miles back to Knaresborough I knew it would be torturous but its only fields and farms id try hit up Lidl see what was left maybe when I got into Knaresborough I start towards the main road and realize I left my water bottle back in the yard and the walkie talkie was broken so I had to find some resources for now their was a small shop in whixley next to the pub id head their to grab some water when I arrived it had already been looted shit I thought and so I headed to the pub ironically I had told the landlord their I would never go back until the end of the world turns out I was right I wander in find a few bottles of j20 and then I see the prize whisky and I jam as much of the spirits in my bag as I can carry even if no one else was able to see the usefulness of having them ill enjoy them I start to head out when the landlord appears he's a zombie but regardless I needed to get back to my settlement to my people and I wanted this piece of shit to suffer a little longer so I side stepped the zombie and headed back out onto the main road I started to walk out of the village when I saw a shadow in the corner of my eye I look to my right there is a little girl in the window but this one is alive not dead so I run to the open door and see a man and a woman both dead I quickly put them down and move their bodies to the side I run up the stairs and nock on the door from where I think iv seen the little girl she runs out of the adjacent room and hugs me she askes if the monsters that had come for mummy and daddy where gone I said yes they have gone she cries where is mummy and daddy I have to answer this one very gently I say I'm afraid mummy and daddy have gone to a better place and one day you will join them their I ask her if she would like to come with me till then she is reluctant at first when she sees the blood dripping from my arm she screams and says ur infected you have been bitten I try to calm her down but she freaks out runs back into the room and slams the door behind her I sit with my back to the wall while I listen to her tears of fear when I reach for the handle she screams so I push into the room and put my hands round her lips at that very second a zombie comes crashing into the house looking for the source of the sound I tell her to hide she cries again I step out in full view of the zombie it runs at me I grab it and throw it through the window behind me it gets back up faster than I was hoping it runs back in and back up the stairs this time I have my knife out and ready I place it by my side it runs I slide it into the side of the zombies head it slumps with a loud thud the little girl comes out and grabs my hand I say to her I'm not one of the monsters she holds onto my hand I pull my jacket down she seas the wound on my arm I tell her it was a bad man who came for me and my people I asked if she wanted to join me while I walk somewhere safe she agrees I ask her to pack up anything she will need food clothes and any medicine I will ask Sarah or Tracy to look after this little one when we get back to Knaresborough I ask if she has a water bottle and any boots as she pulls out some trainers as this hike is not going to be a quick one I also ask if mummy and daddy had a car she shakes her head I ask the little girl her name she says her name is Sophie I introduce myself as ross we set off on foot I am thinking to myself what the hell am I going to do now that remi is dead I put that behind me one obstacle at a time

10:00 A.M

On our way Sophie points out to the animals and to the parts of the road she knows she was only little but she needed to rest more often that I needed to but because she was only little she asked me questions like where was I from was I part of the army I answered them all one at a time I was from Knaresborough however I used to live in whixley and I was not with the army but that a friend of mine was she asked how I got the guns I replied that we went to the army base to pick them up she looked scared when she said some soldiers came to the house trying to bite me I looked at her and realized how scared she really was I gave some of my water as I knew hers was getting low I had lots of j20 in my bag so she had one we then got back on our feet and carried on walking we had walked quiet far since whixley central road I heard a little scream it was Sophie I dropped to one knee swiveled round aimed my gun I looked at her she said she had seen a rat I laughed and stood back up straight but suddenly fear filled my heart if the rats have eaten any of the infected dead they could be infected I asked Sophie to tell me if she saw many of them she said she saw them head back into the fields I told her calmly if you see any more don't scream just hold my hand I shoulder my rifle and I lean in and say squeeze my hand in case you scare them off we need to see if the infection effects them I noticed one shuffling past me I got out a flash that was empty and swiped it up sealed it but left a whole for air figured Karla might need this specimen as we carry on I notice in the field a horde of zombies coming towards us I tell Sophie to get behind me I start picking my targets out and firing one at a time selecting single fire on my M14 one head shot two a few moments later I hear what can only be described as a cannon firing down on the field it erupted into fierce gun fight I saw a unit of soldiers pounding down on them from a helicopter when they hit the deck they where slowly cutting through the crowd that's when I saw him at least I thought it couldn't be .... DAD!!!!!

12:30 P.M

I looked at my father he is still holding the blood stained sword it was a samurai sword he was just tapping it on his feet he then decided it is time to talk I new he was once with the army as a special forces fighter but I thought his time was over I could see the pain in his face I asked after my step mum he said she was safe on one of the islands but that she would be moved back to the main land once his operations where over I told him what we were doing he looked happy that we had kept so many alive I asked him how he got involved he said he had been keeping tabs on the events around the world when shit hit the fan he'd been deployed to the south with his unit barley a squad sized he had called for reinforcements when they refused him the air support he'd pulled back attempting to contact me and nick to hold down and get down to his house it was always dad that wanted me and nick to learn to shoot but mum had always said no to guns I'm surprised I didn't think of that remi would of smacked me on the back of the head for this had he been alive dad looked at Sophie who was sat so close hiding under my arm he spoke to her as he had spoken to me when I was a child with a soft and loving and caring side and asked Sophie hey sweetheart is ross being good to you she didn't answer till I said it was ok that he had stopped the monsters from hurting me and her she eventually spoke up and told him that I found her and saved her again I asked him what the plan was from hear on out he responded by asking me what my plan was I said well I have people to get to your more than welcome to join hell we really need someone like you round to help us survive he spoke to the pilot who swung round and headed for the field close to Knaresborough but It couldn't land so we had to jump out dad told me he would return with Judith and with others within two days giving us time to get settled and build up the new base he couldn't come with us at this point but gave me a message to give to nick I asked if he wanted Sophie to come with me he agreed she would be safe with me so off they went and now I had to deal with the shock of telling remi wife that he had passed once we had waived our way through ally ways and on the road I could see the wall and on it was Scott looking out over he smile and waved at me he could see the sad look on my face and he shouted where is remi I told him to get them to open the door as soon as I stepped in Gemma rushed over to me hugged me remi wife walked up to me and asked where is my husband I said that we needed to chat and pulled her to one side I explained that we got hit by a van it flipped us we where pinned I was unconscious as was remi when I woke he had been turned I told her the zombie that did it was no ash and that I had put my knife into the side of remis head I handed her his dog tags everyone went quiet as we gave a moments silent for the morning widow when she finally stopped crying I went to her and hugged her close she asked if his body could be brought back to the yard I explained that I burnt his body but that I might be able to get some of the ashes for her at a later date nick came in and gave me a hug I handed him the message that dad had given me nick was the eldest in the family he laughed and said that son of a bitch made it who could of guessed his smile was electric but I needed to press for someone to help with Sophie and so I asked Scott and Sarah if they could look out for the little girl once everyone was settled back down I asked for everyone to come to the yard I had something important to discuss when everyone moved out I went up onto the wall to keep watch while I discussed issues with them I announced that my father was alive and was bringing reinforcements at this point Jamie started to smile and laugh that tough son of a bitch still lives he said I explained that the fortress needed to be ready for soldiers and everyone else within the two days after this I stood down and went for some food I was exhausted I could see zombies through the shutters so I kept quiet If they knew we where hear that single door wouldn't hold for very long so I started moving heavy objects into the way it turned faced the door ran at it others soon joined in I realized we needed better doors up after a few minutes the zombies moved on I felt like we where being tested like the zombies knew we where inside I quietly started to cry by myself I felt the huge loss that had occurred over such a short time I cried and cried until nick and mum came in and sat with me we cried together then all at once just started hugging each other we will never forget the fallen I was lucky I had the people I did around me I felt so blessed but so cursed as well I thought about it then realized if the world has gone to shit how many of us were left to fight this chaos I stood up headed for Paul and started cleaning the guns one at a time nick joined me I was going bat shit crazy id had enough if I was going to make a stand this was the moment I was going to re claim some of our homes I loaded up an APC Paul Scott me and nick went out hunting Pete and Reece stood guard in the yard I wanted to get some serious pay back I decided to listen to Paul's advice last second rob jumped on top of the APC with a loaded MP40 a battle cry was given when we where all on our way we moved to the castle unloaded rob and Paul discussed strategy while I 3 behind two kneeling me on front with nick Paul Scott and Rob behind us when we unloaded a clip the three moved forwards and took a kneel rob looked back at the .50 cal and jumped on it started firing we wanted the zombies to find us the more we killed the clearer the streets would be at a later point besides I was sick of hiding if we could clear out a zone we could set up a bigger perimeter and even expand I remember lining up my shots and firing just move and clear when we had cleared the castle we started to head into the market square again move and shoot if they got close call it out when out of no where a group of people joined in coming into eye sight my god these bastards inspired the reaper back out of me they where hand to hand well close enough with swords and metal poles swinging them round like a battle axe I noticed Jamie was with them his precision with the blunt weapons staggers me I didn't realize he worked with my dad and that was how he knew him he was a solider just as his son was more survivors must of seen the yard and come to our aid I wanted to re take the whole town but this was unrealistic at this point as more just came as we cleared them but now we have a common goal survive the nightmare and re build we start to get overwhelmed so I shout to Jamie to take the survivor's back to the house and we would draw them away with the APC he nodded then headed off I blasted my .50 cal barrot into the crowed cutting down three zombies getting all their attention me rob Paul and Scott and nick belted it back to the APC rob jumped on top he started firing with hatred at the zombies id later find out he watched his mum getting eaten and that's why he hated them so dam much we drove round cutting down the horde till it was only a few then sped off in the direction of leaving Knaresborough however made a sharp turn and drove quietly avoiding gathering zombies I noticed something odd their was a zombie child in the middle of the hordes I made a mental note of this as its not the first time iv seen one of these but it's the first time to see a horde around them we finally make it back to the yard its full of people now we are over crowding it but it will hold some of the new comers introduce themselves I asked them all to be as quiet as possible if there are any children or any skilled workers if they would step forward I was in luck half a dozen men stepped forward turned out they where builders that was perfect we needed them to get straight down to Jakub smith field and start helping them build the houses and buildings that where needed I sent Jamie and rob down with them in a van and Paul went for over watch I sent the rest of the parties to help them or to gather materials or food and medicines realizing that this town was starting to be depleted I figured one big group going to Harrogate to gather things might be better as their was camping shops and that meant tents gas and electrical parts that we needed I realized that there was significant more risk going further away so I sent Scott nick and Tracy's husband with them while I stayed back I went to see the medical center to see how they where progressing they had found that the zombie virus mutated every time they attempted to fight it with anti biotics but at least it was an improvement on not knowing anything about it I went to Libby who fixed up my arm again as I had torn the stiches she looked at me as if to say you idiot I jokily said you should see the other guy then I remembered he was literally in the church over the road and my thoughts turned dark again but remembered I had the role of leader now that remi was gone and that I had to be a fair leader and understanding I missed the old times with my friends at that very moment their was a bang on the wall I looked over to the century who said it was human so I opened it up in jumped Steve Dan and Alex my childhood friends Jesus Christ I exclaim where the hell have you all been hiding under a rock or something they all collapse and I get them some help into the yard

7:00 P.M

When Steve finally came round he wanted to chat to me straight away I asked why he told me ben had gone missing I had to gently sit him down and tell him id seen ben die and that he was buried with samie apparently they had been waiting for him to return when he didn't they started looking for him id forgotten they all lived together down on eastfeild one of the estates of knaresborough the town was divided into four estates east field Stockwell aspins and central I lived in central my dad lived on eastfeild and Gemma lived on Stockwell he then said when they couldn't find him they figured they would try hear but didn't dare come close as all the shooting seemed to be coming from hear I laugh at that saying yes that was me my bad I asked if he had seen anyone else he shook his head he didn't even see his parents or any of their parents so he assumed they got out while they could I asked Steve if he had a weapon when he shook his head again I handed him my ball point .22 hunting rifle and asked him to follow me onto the wall we stood side by side as we had many times against the zombies in games however this was real life it was different he was nervous about shooting guns Alex joined us on the wall as did Dan as they picked up pistols I said just like Nazi zombies shoot for the head only difference is fire sparing there is no max ammo this is real life I looked at Dan as he looked so sad I said relax I'm sure this will all be over soon we took aim and fired at the zombies when the last one fell on the ground I said round over hand in ur weapon's to Paul once I stepped down Gemma came up to me and said why did you pretend this was a game I replied well because they are in shock best way to deal with it is to pretend it is while we bring them out of shock then they will be ready for the real thing she nodded and agreed then hugged me again I asked if I could speak to Gemma's father and mother on my own for a moment so Gemma stepped back I pulled Pete to one side and said if and when this ends id like your blessing to marry your daughter it's a tradition in my family to ask the fathers permission Pete considered this and said to me if this is to end then to speak to him later on I agreed now wasn't the time to be asking but he said to me that he felt so proud of me for asking his permission first once everyone was back in I asked for progress of the new site things where moving ahead quicker than they had hopped I asked if their was any problems rob came in covered in mud but in a gilly suit he had fashioned he said not to much activity but enough to keep me busy with the silencer I considered this and asked to go see it on the next day as in two days more should be arriving specialists hopefully everyone sat and ate Sarah finally wandered over to me while I was deep in thought she said this is all because of you I remind her remi was the main reason it happened she looked at me and said no he dealt with the security you organized us I just wanted to say thank you I asked if she minded having all the children around her she used to work with children and that's what I needed her to do she said at times it was difficult at times it was easy but that was part of the job she looked at me and said you seem different that you used to I remember a time when I used to be a clown of the town now it seems I'm running this shit storm of a show that's when I remember the spirits and the rat shit shit shit where is my backpack I get the rat out its still alive luckily I hand it over to Karla she looked like id given her the best present of her life and as for the spirits I divided it three for medical rest for recreational use sheared one with Gemma and sheared a drink I poured out shots and got on the wall asked everyone to raise their shots to remember the fallen at that moment I noticed over the wall a massive horde I mean huge one passing so I jumped off the wall told everyone to be silent as this was a massive horde we could not win this fight everybody falls silent I'm aiming my gun everyone grabs a rifle aiming in a different way it must have been in the thousands of zombies what was drawing them hear I couldn't think straight but their was so many as they passed the APCS a few nocked into them making loud noises I hear a loud thud and I look over the wall this thing looks fucking huge made of muscle could probably jump over the wall it had mutated fuck I thought I slowly crawl up the wall and take a picture with a camera I found so I could show the others what was up against the wall it didn't hear the clicker luckily the horde passes after ten minutes Paul said that he had never thought about it mutating in such a way and that this could not be real when he was shown the picture later on we recognized them as a mutated gene that was made by the virus again a large explosion I looked it was one of the petrol stations we had rigged so at least we knew where they would be headed so no operations down that way tonight I realized we might need to make a run back up to the army base or even head out to York to raid their stockpile.

Day four: we built it so hear they come

6 A.M

I woke to seeing Gemma staring out of the window looking down at all the zombies shuffling past I realize this must be so difficult for her as all her family and friends lived in Knaresborough I am so grateful her parents and grandmother made it to us but as far as the rest no sign our group is bigger now than when we began its rather nice to know we are not alone in surviving this nightmare and knowing that my dad was rallying troops to come to our aid when I walked down the stairs I was met by nick and my mum looking worried in my direction I slowly walk down nick pulls me to the side and mentions the fact that we were running short on ammunition and he looked as If he had seen a ghost I turned to fast but caught myself before falling over this is a classical move of mine in the morning all I could do was grab the wall as I spun round it was Scott how had he snuck up on me I look at him Sarah is with him both of them are white as ghosts I ask what is wrong its josh he's gone I looked at them seriously and asked what do you mean he is gone

Sarah spoke up and said he must of got out of the yard I panic as if he can get out they can get in but then I think why haven't we seen any up to this point I decide to go out looking for him Scott wants to join me but I ask him to remain with Sarah as he is too close to this his judgment would be clouded so I set out alone thinking he went to the school close by Jesus id forgotten that it was a school day when all this had happened and so glad josh was off sick so I head in with my knife no loud noises fuck knows what's waiting for me its places like hospitals and schools that always gave me the shivers it's also the school I went to so I figured I knew my way around it had been 10 years since I left king James school I know that josh likes his games so I head to the i.t rooms at the front of the school no such luck he's not hear I remember talking to him one day while I sat at Scotts house we laughed and played games me Scott and josh if I remember correctly it was watch dogs man he was an ace hacker in the game but I schooled him on black ops zombies I started feeling like I wasn't alone in this school I saw blood stains all over the doors and all over the floor where it looked like people had been dragged away I finally head down to the fields behind king James as it seems if he was deeper inside he would end up out hear just as I sat down on the field I saw him running towards me I think ah finally he has made his senses back then I see close behind him a horde of zombies fuck I wish I had brought my gun and he's running straight to me he looked so scared fair play to him id of been afraid if I was him he bails past me I realize I wasn't paying attention to my surroundings we made for the wall of the grave yard and bailed over it and hid behind it I covered his mouth I felt their presence lots of them small children and teachers trying to track us we had lost them temporarily then they were distracted by something in the distance once I was confident that we were not the focus I looked over the wall turns out a little old lady was being chomped on at the bottom of the hill poor old lady didn't know what hit her I thought about it if this was all there was left the sports gyms would be empty we could get more blunt weapons so I asked for joshes help to carry some of them such as hockey sticks cricket bats and javelins he happily grabbed as many as he could carry that's when it hit me in the back nocking me over I pull out my knife but its thrashing wild and out of control I managed to grip this bastards head and shouted to josh to get the hell out and run back he doesn't hesitate at least if he was safe my life wouldn't of been ended in vain at this point it was just me and it wrestling on the floor me trying desperately to get my knife out it trying to bite me I thought it had made contact with my arm when I realized my arm was bleeding from my arm for fucks sake I thought to myself as I was preparing to strike the zombie I slammed my knife into the side of its head it slumped and then I heard a loud roar and with that it was time for me to get out I legged it outside I didn't realize I was leaving a blood trail after me and that anything could follow me I made it back out onto the field I saw the biggest maddest zombie I'd ever seen shit I had to hide and hide now there was no way I could win in a fight against this one so I hid in the graveyard once again only this zombie was faster and able to track not like all the zombies id seen before it was on me within seconds I pulled out the hockey stick wacked it and tried to pun it cornered me I had nowhere to go I thought shit this is the end for me when out of nowhere I hear a bang and the zombie drops behind him I see nick shaking behind he looked so scared he dropped to his knees and was sick I walked over to him so proud but at the same time so worried for him we walked back to the compound together when I got back Scott thanked me so much for finding his son he asked if there was anything he could do I asked him to keep an eye on josh and to ask him not to do that again Scott assured me he wouldn't let him out of his sight I asked to speak to josh on my own once it was just the two of us I sat him down and grabbed out a gaming computer with loaded in Minecraft he was so happy but it was our secret and not to tell anyone about it other than Sarah and Scott he ran straight up to Scott and apologized for what he had done and that he had been selfish at that exact moment mum Gemma and everyone else came to my side I explained about what I had seen a few looked terrified Jamie and rob seemed like they were excited about these new zombies I was very worried as it was a tracking zombie to this day I am haunted by the first few days and even weeks of the zombie uprising there was just so much carnage and chaos that nobody could keep up with it all after all the commotion settled down I hear a loud roar another one of the big mother fuckers I don't have a clue where they are coming from but they seemed to be focused on us right now I do a quick head count and realize I can't see nick I ask if anybody had seen him no one had I hear the roar again only this time closer and I can hear gunshots getting even closer I look over the wall and see one baring down on nick what the fuck was he thinking of going out on his own that's when Jamie jumped over the wall battle axe in hand smashing it down on the zombies neck rob jumps over to and tag teams his dad in killing the zombie when they look down they see nick with pure panic in his face I jump over the wall landing on all the undead that are close by I see why he is white in the face he's been cut by one of these fuckers he tries desperately to cover it up I think well maybe there could be a cure or possibly we are immune I drag nicks ass back into the yard mum saw nick and burst into tears she starts crying so loud I fear the zombies will hear us Jamie and rob stay out and go for a run to try distract them I take him down into the labs I drag Karla to one side and ask how the cure is coming along she looks at me as if to say are you kidding that's when she sees nicks arm and realizes why I am asking she looks sympathetically into my eyes and says ross you need to be prepared for the worst case scenario I sit with nick for the remaining time I can before they inject him with an attempt to save him I make mum leave me and nick on our own I can tell it isn't working and that it is killing him slowly he looks at me fear in his eyes then all of a sudden he is gone fuck me Karla hugs me but its too late for him I turn round nick is lying motionless on the ground he started to twitch I knew at this point it was too late for him I grabbed my gun and shattered it down onto his skull it exploded into a sea of red all over my face was my brothers blood within seconds he went from alive to undead to dead it all happened so dam fast tears in mine and my mums eyes start to fall fast I'm not a believer in god but if there was and is a god I hope he takes good care of nick until we all join him I start to roar I can't take this shit anymore it's just too much for me to deal with I walk upstairs from the cellar everyone is gathered in the yard I walk past them back into my house silence is complete I get up to my room smash my door closed and break down why the fuck did he jump back out there what was he trying to do mum walks in closes the door and falls to the ground in a flood of tears I realize that what has happened cannot be undone

10:00 A.M

I finally re surface with mum from my room after we had calmed down I still furious partly at the zombies partly at nick for getting himself killed when I get to the yard there is one more duty I must do the same as I did for my sister I must burn the body I climbed onto the pile of wood when I realize Jamie is stood beside me as is Gemma fuck everyone's hear I set the wood on fire using nicks zippo from when we were younger I spoke for a few minutes about the importance of family and that since the event has happened we have no choice but to all be one family I started to think about my dad his promise and spoke firmly and loudly that the FOB had to be finished ASAP I said I'd be positioned on over watch while construction was taking place and that Gemma and Sarah would help support my mother and the children to deal with this traumatic experience I needed time to heal so being alone seemed like the best answer for me so we set off me with my .50 cal ready on the mounted gun to seriously lay into the undead if they showed their face and god did I hope they would we made it down to the FOB (forward operations base) I then got myself to the top of the hill so I could see for miles away I turned the radio down and put a headphones in and started listening to music to calm myself down it is one of the only evidence of nicks pictures I just zoned out for a few moments I looked down the site of the barrot .50 cal I saw a horde wandering past but not in the direction we where working in then I saw them turn I saw a child among them I saw this before I cant believe it I was right I aim for the head of the zombie child I fire I watch its head explode then I watch the zombies start to rage up scattering in all directions a few in our directions I pull out the headphones and turn round see loads of zombies crawling up the hill behind me I grab the walkie talkie shout that I need support Jamie came running up the hill as did rob we took aim as we had the high ground Jamie barks that this is as far as they come we do not hesitate to join in the rally call one of the APCS pulls up behind us the other is on the gate at the other end stationed to protect our escape route and our other people keep working very weary of the impending doom I'm burning with rage I grab a grenade and throw it regardless of the consequences of my actions I lose it throw down the gun pull out my combat knife and run at them thinking back to that moment I'm proud of myself but at the same time so disappointed that I didn't think it could cause me any harm I can hear Jamie scream that's the spirit ross go for it they drop their weapons and join in the carnage the APC stops firing for fear that it would hit us but kept its aim on the further zombies when suddenly the zombies turned and ran away it all of a sudden dawns on me why would they run away unless a new leader had been found fuck it I thought live to fight another day I killed a few of the stragglers taking my sweet time with the zombies that I had I then dragged their bodies to the walls and with help from Jamie and rob threw them over the wall it wasn't pretty but it had to be done to keep the infection out after this we pored fuel onto the bodies and set them on fire I head back to the top of the hill take up my position aiming down the site putting my music back on a bit of breaking Benjamin the halo song when I was younger it was my favorite song I remember playing halo with nick and a few of his friends as I was the younger annoying brother who always wanted to do what he did I remember several days I played when he was busy doing work and him coming in seeing me plasma gunning some grunts then reality hit me hard this wasn't the world it was before I came crashing back to life when the phone died if I got a chance id try to charge it off a generator later on but for now back to watching over the crowed working to build up the FOB in the distance I could see explosions from Harrogate I wondered what was happening their I heard Libby over the radio I thought that was weird so I tuned into the station she was just checking up on me and the rest to make sure it wasn't us causing the fires I spoke up when Jamie was about to reply with nothing to do with us and not to worry probably some looters or survivors trying to burn their way out and that we are not to concern ourselves about it that's when the helicopters arrived down the rope my father descended in all his glory I was seriously impressed after him followed at least forty men and women I saw Judith his wife when dad looked for me he couldn't see me as I was gullied up I was walking to him when he pulled his sword out and put it towords my neck I removed the hood and he put the sword down saying never sneak up on an old man I laughed he asked me where nick was I spoke softly and gently not to make him angry but to give him sympathy once he knew what had happened he broke down and began to scream and shout he looked more full of rage than I had done earlier that day it had only been a few hours since I had smashed his skull in I fight back the tears I look to my father who is openly crying I cry with him he blames himself for not being hear for us I blame myself as I couldn't control his actions when Judith slaps both of us and snaps us out of it I lock heads with my dad and tell him we will burn every single one of these zombie fucks until no more dare come near us the helicopters lands and people start to unload all the equipment that's when I notice the horde coming in from the rear fuck I shout dad looks at Jamie and rob then at me they join me on top of the hill we kill and slice and dice these mother fuckers none get past me and dad fighting with guns knives and swords we swing for what feels like only a few moments but it had been hours I guess it was the adrenaline and the fuel for battle and the hunger to do damage to these when we finish dad looks at me and goes well you must be one of mine only rage that my family and my blood suffers he chuckles and wipes his sword off a few other soldiers join us he orders them to stand down and that the fight had already been won they looked

disappointed I remind them there will be plenty of
fighting to come I asked a few to go with Jamie to the
compound and gather everyone and bring them down
here now that there is more of us we can survive while
we build one of the APCS goes with them since we had
this area covered I decided I'd go have a look at how
they seem to be getting in I find a small gate id never
noticed before wide open so I get one of the engineers
to build a make shift fortification we would have to get
it sorted more permanently however for now it would
do we would need a century hear too so I post a few of
the fresh soldiers to guard it I didn't care really as long
as this was the only place they could get in I was rather
annoyed with the lads who found this area and left out
this great weakness once everyone is down at the FOB
and the yard is deserted I want to get a ride up and
spend a bit of time alone in the house I drive up to the
yard it feels like before when I used to set off to work
and it would be silence it was so nice yet so horrible at
the same time I knew this wasn't going to last forever
and I knew we wouldn't of held them hear looking at
the state of the wall I'm amazed it lasted its been
beaten to the point it nearly collapsed so grateful we
were out of their I'm so glad mum was safe or safer
than she would have been hear I walk around the
empty houses I look at all the photos of mum nick me
and friends I cry quietly as I no I'm alone but can hear
shuffling outside I go up to my room grab my bow and
all other weapons that I had gathered over time I knew

I couldn't leave just yet id have to wait for them to pass that's when I saw the yard door open and zombies come flooding in thank god we got out of here they all look so confused that nobody is hear except me they notice me in the shadows and start running after me I leg it up the stairs thinking fuck fuck fuck how the hell am I going to get out of here now I slam doors behind me but they keep pushing forward I turn and face them with the wall by my side I don't really remember why I stopped but I stood so still and calmly that's when it happened when I blacked out…….

2:00 P.M

I regained consciousness covered in blood all the bodies cut to pieces around me I quickly check my entire body for a bite mark I sigh with relief when I realize I am not bit how the hell did this happen I look down the corridor blood all over the walls zombies or what whatever these fuckers are they came to close to my loved ones killed my family and friends it was my turn to get pay back on these monsters only four days it's taken me to become the warrior that I guess I was supposed to be its taken brothers sisters and all of humanity to make me this good at killing I look up and see the security camera that dad had set up the second id turned 16 to protect me and my brothers I can see its still alive if ever I'm going to know what happened hear id have to hook this up to a computer josh he had the computer I needed I grab the CCTV camera and head back to the yard there is so many dead zombies I really need to watch this CCTV footage to see what I did I headed for the car jumped in and drove straight back to the encampment I see zombies in the shadows shuffling away from the road as I drive past not even trying to attack the car I feel weird and watched almost like it's a trap I decide to drive round for a while I hear gun fire I decide its time to go back to the camp as I approach the zombies back away from the gate I drive past running a few of them over as I go but they seem to be no combatant my dad looks at them then at me driving towards him confused in all my years I have never seen him look so confused I swing the car round jump out with my blades drawn right to his side he smiles seeing my uniform covered in blood he looks at me and says been busy have we I look at him and reply no doubt this isn't my blood you no he looks weary of that comment even though he knows I'm joking he has seen too much blood recently and is very worried the zombies seem to pull back and withdraw again he looks confused he turns to me and says either you are the luckiest charm or we need to have a serious chat with that I'm surrounded and guns are pointing at me I fall week and collapse the last thing I hear before I'm completely under is mum and Gemma screaming when I come to I'm tied to a chair the CCTV camera is hooked up and dad Is sat next to me watching the footage he seemd to be studying it replaying it when I finally get my senses back he looks darkly into my eyes I knew I had been bad but fuck me the footage showed me tearing them apart limb from limb using anything to my advantage he looks impressed with my combat skills that is until I start to glow and moving quicker and faster than any of them could ever see coming I smirk no wonder they fear me he turns and looks me dead in the eyes and asks if this has ever happened before I answer honestly and reply that no of course not he looks even darker the doctor comes in and takes a blood sample I give it willingly the needle feels sharper than it should once they have taken it and checked they can't see the zombie gene he cuts the ropes and asked if we can have a chat in private I answer of course he looks at me and says not you numb nuts and looks at the doctors they all withdraw from the room he sits with me quietly for a moment then asks if I knew anything about the family history and anything of our origins I answer no so he asked if nick had shown me the message id responded no he didn't as he really didn't once he had herd that he praised to the sky to a man in the sky sorry I shouldn't mock but after all I've seen a god doesn't seem realistic he turned to me and said nick was protecting you as you're a forth gen fighter there are only six or seven of us alive at any one time and when danger is present that we would all link up and fight the oncoming storm it flows through the blood line of the same family it has done since ancient times I look at my dad as if he was crazy but the way he looked at me then I asked if nick was one he replied no and that nick was ordered to protect me in case I was a forth I asked who the others where he responded he didn't know and that only a family with pure intentions and heart were chosen I was like yer that's got to be bullshit he smacks me behind the head I laugh he laughs the doctors come back in see us laughing on the ground and just sigh Libby is outside alongside all of the people my dad steps to the side and shows me im not glowing anymore so that's good I guess Gemma steps up beside me I speak clearly and determined I say the zombie horde I dealt with in the house was a trap and that zombies are getting smarter they must have a leadership so we needed to follow hordes and needed to call out targets I also brought out the t.v from the tent I ask for the film to be played my dad looks at me to say are you seriously wanting them to no I reply everyone has a right to see this masterpiece and everyone deserves to have their say when the video starts they all stare at me and then the screen in awe Jamie looks at me like a god of chaos and mayhem it's almost like a look of pure love I laugh and say maybe one day it will happen again but till that day I will not rest till the zombie hordes are on their knees or beneath the ground I rally a call to arms with an unknown power they all are willing to follow me into battle only a few don't believe the footage and think its faked I ask how they think I could fake such a thing as they are looking at me I'm glowing and moving round harnessing the power that must have been unlocked by the horde from before I move faster and faster they seem to believe it now ha-ha I laugh I stop when I look up they are all kneeling in front of me I refuse to let them we are all human I bow to all of them as all men and woman are equal only thing I won't bow to is zombies fuck them no mercy for them I run out the gate grab one of the nearest zombies and drag it in in front of the group I smash it in half I look displeased with the result but it has the desired effect on the group

8:00 p.m.

I'd been thinking since earlier that maybe there is others with the ability like me and if so had they survived the horrors of this apocalypse my dad stepped up and spoke I have let him take charge as I needed some space after finding out about my abilities I needed time to come to terms with it and how and why my body glows when I use it either way the fortifications where up and running I made sure dad was left in charge as I walked round the walls edge looking for potential weak spots I noticed a few cracks I called for some of the soldiers to protect it while the repairs are made I needed some time away from all the responsibilities a few people had packed up and left since finding out about my abilities they didn't feel comfortable to be honest I didn't blame them I didn't even no what I was capable of I decided to waste no more time in finding out I went looking for one of the big sons of a bitches no time to waste it didn't take me long one was hammering on the wall at the back of the land we had picked I dived onto the wall and then onto its back I summond all of my strength and smashed into its skull it split into a thousand pieces sending blood and brains all over the place a few soliders cheered and kept fireing if only they new what it was that lurked inside me they would of begged me to go faster and to cut right to the thick of the ranks I hadn't seen any of the children in ages I remembered remi and how much I missed him I returned to the center of the encampment I saw remis wife and son I saw Scott Sarah josh I saw Gemma I saw all of the friends and strangers that where hear they looked at me as I passed libby ran up to me and checked me over seeing all the blood I was covered in I assured her it wasn't mine and that it was the zombies still she wanted to check just to make sure I plugged my headphones in I wanted to zone out I didn't care that I was covered after all that had happened in such a short space of time we had been to hell and back each of the people deserved to be left in peace as they had survived the horrors we still had so much to learn from the undead I decided to sit on top of the hill and just have a few moments to myself I finally got hit hard by all the loss my family had seen my poor sister my brother I no that was only a small loss to the rest of the human race but to me it was the worst thing to happen in the whole world I didn't want the loss of their lives to hold me back but the tears poured down my face I was loosing a battle not outside my body but inside it I sat their for what felt like hours however it was only a short time when I looked up I saw my dad sat by my side watching the sun set I think he was keeping a close eye on me didn't want to loose me to my own mind he said to me in the kindest of words burry that sadness take it out on the undead they are the reason we have lost so much I looked my dad straight in the eyes with tears in both our eyes I spoke softly asked him if while he was back with the army they knew anything of the origins of the virus he said that if I felt ready he would talk to me with what he had learned I replied that I was calm he spoke of a prophecy of the world being brought to its knees and that a few would rise and take control either to end it or to save it I looked at him again like he was crazy and said under my breath saying whats worth fighting for this world is being ravaged more and more each day it seems the hords are getting smarter and stronger as time progresses the billions of people who were now either dead or undead only small pockets of life left I said to dad is this really caused by us or is this caused by a god a cruel god that's when he hit me round the head and reminded me of the truth im still alive proving im worth keeping round I hear the APC firing I look at dad and tell him to go and that I would keep over watch on all the land unused by us and make sure nothing broke through

I then hear a shudder on the ground like a earth quake I see seven of them big fuckers I decide enough is enough I leave the top of the hill I use the speed and agilituse the speed and agility I poses to my advantage I push much faster the zombies back off but the bigger ones focus on me asif im nothing one swats me aside like im a fly I fall unconscious for a few moments and when I come to im surrounded by the big fuckers they waited for me to regain myself before pounding down on me I took hit after hit but refused to falter I could hear Gemma screaming my name in the background as they tried to claw their way to me I look at them I get smashed so hard I fly back into the wall thinking this is it that's when they arrived ....

Day five: the arrival of the fourths legends or destroyers

Once they hit the deck it was so amazing like they were falling directly from the sky I saw them land with a thud behind them the ground shook five angel like figures with swords and guns attached to their sides smashing the zombies into the dust raise up and start fighting as chaos erupted around me I came to my senses and started joining in almost instinctively like we were one and the same as the fighting came to an end they looked up at the remaining zombies I rushed them destroying them in mear seconds the armor these people were wherein it was so impressive but they all wore masks each had a different design my father stepped up and tried to shake their hands knowing who they are they ignored him and grabbed me by the neck picked me back up he took a step back at that moment there was a crash I felt pressure build but then lift straight away I look down I see that I'm now in one of the suits all I can see of my father is a proud man he knew I was meant to be one of them he just didn't think he would live to see me suited up my suit reminded me of space marines from Warhammer 40 k I used to play the strategy game when I was younger the one that had picked me up spoke to me with a strong accent he seemed to be from the south of the country I listened as carefully as possible it was hard to understand but what i got was that I was to paint it with whatever colors that I wanted I was so excited I new exactly what I wanted blue and black with gold trim that it already had on it I drew a white rose with my knife into it to represent Yorkshire only the greatest county of all in England again my father tried to engage them into a conversation there response was that they came for me to help in their war and that the small battles were already lost I refused I refused to abandon all that I stood for im not the leader of this team but I have my right to refuse one of them Gabriel tried to reason with me saying that the entire of human life itself required us to fight for it I remain stubborn till three of the fourths leave two remain with me trying to explain that they had already lost quite a few fourths and that there may never be many more I still stand my ground I won't ignore my people and so they stay with me to help clean up the mess we made my father looks at me with pride as we walk back in the armor vanishes into thin air the fourths look like ordinary teenagers I seem to be the oldest one it felt weird but people looked at the new fourths one of them is a skinny teenager she looked a lot more fierce in the armor I usher them into my hut and ask for the story in more detail about what they know I learn their names one is called Beth the other is Kyle from what they gathered this war has been raging for many century's never had evil taken this form however the suits appear once the abilities have activated and when you're in danger they came as they sensed me being beaten into the ground and in their code of conduct they must protect each other to the best of their abilities my father finally stepped in and kyle and beth both apologized for the behavior of the other fourths something about being around people really upset them as it reminded them of what they had lost beth seemed to be the most affected by it when dad had finished asking his questions about the plan and if their was anything we could do I reminded him I was remaining where I was this is were my fight is beth respected that and so did kyle he had kept very quiet that's when Gemma ran in grabbing me and hugging me close I introduced her she thanked them for saving my life I could feel they were blushing from it even though their orders where to save me at all costs I ask if they wanted to stay with us and help us win the fight hear they agreed for now to help me learn about my abilities at this point I didn't no that the suits enabled them to fly had I of realized this id of asked for help in that first it took me at least three weeks to master flight but that's not what I needed to learn first it took so long to summon the suit again when I did I summoned it in front of me so I could spray paint it I asked why we were called the fourths they asked why my nickname was reaper I showed them a clip from when I played games of zombies they laughed gemma grabbed me by the hand lead me to her tent today she wanted something only I could give her a massive cuddle and kisses I then had other jobs to attened to but she reminded me about the promise I had made her that morning I laugh and head out to do training beth and kyle had summoned their armour and dragged some zombies in from outside the wall showing off their skills with swords bare fists and guns the size of a barrot 50 cal but they where only the hand guns for these guys I was so impressed the other fourths kept on appearing until the full squad was lined up practicing when gabrial finally landed he laughed joined the line stood next to me swords drawn as they finish the final move he made a battle cry all the other fourths followed suit once the unit sat down we exchanged stories turns out Gabriel was left for dead in Scotland no one was coming to his aid then in a flash his suit surrounded him keeping him from the horde he watched his entire clan being killed and so he separated himself from his humanity when I explained what happened hear he realized my dad was only trying to be polite earlier and wasn't trying to trap him he turned to my dad asked him to come join the circle as my dad knew about the fourths more than anyone else knew eventually the whole camp was talking to the fourths even to me asking if the armor was heavy my father told them what he had told me that the choice was theirs to make good or bad they are to try save the human race Gabriel put his wall back up but didn't budge as he wanted to be part of the unit and didn't want to be alone again today although it has been a long day I just wanted to sleep but I doubted that would happen out of the corner of my eye I saw two of the children zombies I stand they run as soon as they realized they had been noticed I give chase but they move to fast and sacrifice their zombie guards

5:00 p.m

Iv been chasing the zombies as far as I can that's when I see the horror that beholds me a mounting of corpses fresh not old enough to notice them from before its in the town center it wasn't that long ago that I was there I suit up other fourths land nearby we go back to back covering ever angle it stepped out a zombie not like the rest bigger than what I thought was the biggest zombie out their clearly I was wrong Gabriel looked concerned one of the fourths ran at it out of nowhere it had an axe in its hand it decimated one of the fourths all of a sudden the pain in the air was like we all suffered at the same time we felt a pain unlike any other before it I run at it screaming all the other fourths follow suit only six of us remain now I smash into it barging it with my shoulder it stunned gets knocked back but gets up quicker than I can react as im about to smash into it again it stops me dead in my track and speaks like human language that stuns me I remember the words it spoke it said I see the fourths are not as legendary as I was told as a child clearly the wrong batch has been brought forward as a challenge at that moment I scream kicking it in the face it knocks over

Day 6: The devil among man

2:00 A.M

We fought for hours and hours with this monster trying to finish it but every time we made advances it just out stepped us it was 2 A.M exhaustion was taking over I realized we had been dealing no damage so I stop Gabriel stops too and so do the rest this monster speaks again saying now that play time is over I need to speak to you as you are not fighting for the right reasons he says even though he is clearly one of them I'm to exhausted to try stop him from talking the armor disappears it doesn't stop me from ignoring what he's saying he wants us to turn our back on humanity two of the fourths start to pant as they are our of breath he turns to them tuts at them almost taunting us to break rank but we remain its at this point a marksman from the settlement takes a shot he must have been sent by dad to keep watch he kept firing not realizing zombies are surrounding him I call to him he ignores me and keeps shooting I see them dragging his body backwards all I can imagine after that is the gruesome sounds he was making as they killed him ripping him apart limb from limb his head is thrown off the building again seen as a taunt I look at the zombie in front of us and I said to him are you the devil because I don't believe in any god he laughs at that and says no man is the devil not him he is only hear because they needed leadership Gabriel looks at it and says your kind has taken everything from me I killed one of your brothers up in Scotland and will do the same to you that stops this monster laughing I shout at him get to the point so we can kill you and have this over and done I wanted to fight but had no energy to fight he knew it so did I it was all talk no fight part of me wishes id of listened to what he was saying but part of me knew he was talking shit to try turn us on our own kind it wasn't going to happen I remember looking down to my right id left a sign post with a sharp end sticking into the ground id had enough of listening I ripped it out of the ground and threw it at it it hit it in the head like all the other zombies it went to the ground it was dyeing I ran over to it and smashed its skull into the ground that's when I heard a howl and a whisper from behind me the monster was laughing killing me loses control over the hordes the exact second this happened our Armor appeared we were all geared up again I jumped as did the others when I crashed down it was a massive area of dust blew up underneath my feet the zombies under me where crushed by the sheer force the massive fuckers appeared hundreds of them that's when I saw helicopters APCS every fucking thing this was now a war zone we were on the front line and fighting with a new found energy the horde just kept appearing it seemed like it was never going to end when the horde finally started to die off I could feel the ground shaking I knew what was happening the big fuckers had rallied the fourths had a job to do so we stood in the line pulled out the swords attached to the armor started swiping at them when fighter jets got involved they took out the zombies on the outskirts of the town almost like this was the warzone that was worth fighting I clock my dad on a raideo I see zombies headed straight for him he doesn't even look bothered pulls out his sword and starts in with all the other soliders I see parachuts opening in the sky this is definatly a co-ordinated attack I smile and wave them forward the fourths split off and lead their own attacks

6A.M

After hours and hours of fighting we finally pull back and let the APCS tear them apart with the jets and helicopters giving us a chance to rest for a while we get back to the encampment when we get back I collapse gemma runs over to me sees that im bleeding she grabs libby but its to late Gabriel is already dealing with it from all the fighting the body has exhausted itself libby takes a look at the wound takes swabs to make sure no infection had gotten inside of the wound beth and kyle ask if there is any water for a shower I respond that there is but by that point they had already been directed by someone to where the water was dad rushes to my side I ask why he sent a sole sniper to protect us when he asks where he is I say that zombies got him dad shudders but it doesn't faze him I ask where all that fire power came from and why it came to our aid dad responded that the battle was clearly important and that the army had fallen just small emounts of militia remained fighting for those who he worked for before turns out they want to support the fourths but he couldn't tell me what they wanted with us he said that they wanted to survive and the best chance was by our side so he had called them in by chopper they landed with medical supplies and ammo and food while the fighting was taking place we all shear a common goal to survive in this dark world maybe with the fourths there is still a light to survive I head back to the top of the hill the other fourths join me after a shower the sunlight is raising behind us from a distance this must have looked impressive as we all line up the armour disappears the helicopters land the planes head back to their base to re fuel and re supply till we have enough space for them my wounds have been patched up I swore as soon as the armours gone I look like a zombie I'm starving I realized I haven't eaten in nearly two days I sit down and the others join Gabriel Kyle Beth me and two others who don't shear their names I don't press as it is every persons right the squad looked worried about what the monster had said to them it felt like we didn't kill it that we just slowed it down I assured them I put my foot on its skull and made sure its brains were gone still the feeling was unsettling that it was able to move so quickly that why did it let me kill it I didn't raise this concern to the others as I was worried it would make them panic I hear a tank role up into the field more survivors and soldiers I decided to speak about it to the others I want the soldiers to get involved and don't want them to feel like we are taking over they have an equal say in the fight for the human race so I decided that once we have rested for a few hours that we would convene in my hut no armor rank mattered however we were the power house behind the movement dad would be in control of the army and its input I would be in control of the fourths this was agreed by the fourths as this is where I was from I went to walk around the perimeter the zombies were no longer their it was odd there was always one or two but it seemed like their plan had been changed like they were ordered to back off the area I thought we had cut the head off the snake but this just made my worst fears come to life maybe the thing I killed I didn't actually kill I only took one head off the hydra and two more had sprouted I saw very little movemt so I decided to get some rest till the time I was required

12:30 P.M

I woke fast the sound of movement woke me up I heard a tap at the door I opened it gently I saw little sophie the girl I found in the house she had some flowers in her hand she had braided a bracelet from them and handed them to me I put it on and smile she gave me a big hug and then wandered off I headed back inside to get dressed properly back into my camo gear I wanted to appear normal Scott Sarah Tracy traces husband and children Gemma followed me Gemma's dad and mum my mum Libby dad a few commanding officers joined in Reece and all the rest carried on with their work I got to the microphone and started to speak I needed some water for the first time in a while I grabbed a bottle of water then tried to speak again this time more clearly I spoke of the fact that the fourths where hear for the protection of the survivors and that they would help no matter what the cost I remind them all that this wouldn't work if people fell behind I reminded everyone of the sacrifices that had to be made to get to this point I reminded everyone of remis sacrifice and how proud he would have been had he scan what we had become little Sophie ran up to me and held my hand and Gemma held my other hand I had a tear of sadness in my eyes but whipped them away no place for sadness while there was work to be done and till we figure out a cure or the zombies are eliminated from the entire world we would keep fighting on every second counts after this I went to the newly built strategy and planning area must have been built while I slept Gemma went back to organizing the hunt for further food equipment and other outside the walls events before I got to the tent I saw Paul he was cleaning riffles and organizing ammo he explained that we had enough for an army I explained we had an army now he laughed and chatted as we walked to the area once I was there I could see everyone was waiting for me I apologized for being late they waved it off the war was needing to be fought but exhaustion would have killed us all my worst fears had been confirmed that we had cut the head off a hydra and it had raised a new leader to the replace the one I killed and it was pissed off with me apparently that's when we hear a massive smash at the front wall its collapsed the APCS are firing like no man's business there is a massive Horde pounding in rushing in without hesitation all the fourths armors raised the soldiers pounded them as hard as they could we joined the battle smashing them back crushing them taking their heads off and slicing them in half I could see the lads firing their guns over the walls I was so proud of them at this point they had excepted what was happening in the world and made it work for them the weather was awful not only was it windy it was raining first time in days im so worried about gemma and about everyone else I cant belive that within six days all this has happened I feel lucky to have made it this far a zombie throws itself at me I catch it mid air slam it into the ground it explodes red flies everywhere its blood soaking the ground it will be cleaned up eventually I look thinking fuck this shit I push forwards as do the fourths I see it it looks me dead in the eye it throws itself forward for all to see it's the same fucker that I killed it smiles at me I hear it say did you really think it would be that easy to kill me it moved with such speed it caught me off guard what it wasn't expecting was that Gabriel had seen this before he landed on top of it smashing it with his boot he then dropped a WP grenade on its head forced it into the body of it I could see it squirming underneath him desperately trying to get it out of it but it was too late with a white flash it burnt from the inside out the zombies all launch out a full on retreat back to the state of the start zombies stupid creatures not knowing what to do having no leader again Gabriel set fire to the corps of the zombie overlord he looked over and said sorry I should of warned you to kill them it's really hard not impossible just difficult but something still doesn't feel right I turn round and see what horrified me a zombie was biting into dads neck I run at it grabbing it sending it flying off into the distance dad looks at me panicking he tells me to return to the fight I drag him off the battle field I take him to the medical wing they quarantine him I can see him shaking not nervously he knows he's fucked he sits down I sit with him all of a sudden the zombies pull back and disappear into the midday sunlight all the fourths come to my side see my dad sat on a chair with bite marks all over his neck and legs naturally he should of turned by now but he's a tough son of a bitch Judith runs in but I hold her back as he's bitten I want to hope he's immune but I can tell the virus is taking control he's losing the fight he asks me for a moment alone with him everyone else leaves once the room is clear he says this was a tactic to slow us down by taking something you care and turning into his weapon he has time to take other things from you piece by piece I see him really struggling he's coughing up blood I start to cry he says no tears aloud only anger he then pulls out the sword and asks me not to let him turn into one of them fuckers I can't understand to start with what he wants me to do I don't want to understand but I know what he's implying he starts to growl ordering me to do it I raise the blade up above my head I say to him rest in peace he says see you in hell I said already there and swing slicing through his head taking it clean off the body collapses to the ground motionless I stand next to him and say go to haven where you belong you sick son of a bitch I can hear Judith crying and wailing outside there is literally nothing I can do to ease the pain iv lost so much too I just hold her telling her he died knowing she was safe

9 P.M

I decide that dad would prefer to be burned rather than buried so I gather the whole populous of our area we gather all of fallen heroes a few soldiers from his squad passed by being bitten or ripped apart I look for Gemma but I can't seem to find her I need her so badly she turns up just before I give a speech as I stand I say I'm sick of losing people I'm sick of giving speeches these men deserve our respect and love for giving their lives to keep the rest of us alive I ask if anyone wanted to say anything to our fallen comrades no one comes forward Gemma holding back the tears knowing how hard this is for me after burning my sister my brother and now my father it would be more than my mind could take but being broken like this all I could do is light the torch pass it to Judith and stand with her as the bodies burn I raise a lantern that had been found light it and send it on its way I see things moving in the shadows but I no its friendly as its not attacking it was Gabriel he was wanting to apologies to Judith for not being able to save him I didn't hold it against him this is a war between the living and the dead I usher him to the side and remind him that Judith is morning the loss of her husband they are setting up consoling stations I advise Judith to go to it to get some support that was the last straw I wanted to take back Knaresborough for good I wanted people to feel safe enough to stay in houses again I took it upon myself to go after the fuckers that did this not today but soon enough I was determined I guess this is what dad would have wanted me to do to take back our homes and reclaim our lives I know as a fourth id never live a normal life again but maybe I could return everyone else's life to normality or at least something close to it

Day seven: taking back the streets one by one

7 A.M

Bright and early no rest for the wicked I decided yesterday enough was enough I was going to start cleaning up the streets rather than just kill and abandon them ill tear them apart then clear the area secure them and move people back into the houses first task is getting out the gate at the front as the wall collapsed the engineers are repairing the walls were they can and the builders are doing the best they can I decided I would get all the fourths to help out I know this isn't their fight and I'm grateful they have stayed with us for this long I guess we are like a pack refusing to abandon each other another fourth rose out of the area so Gabriel had to go collect the person and bring them back so he was out of the way for a while so I decided to press on I figured I'd clear out the roads close by extend the perimeter bit by bit the houses close by were burnt out but the ones further down the road were all livable however likely that zombies where inside them so I cleared the first livable ones I wanted to make sure the doors could be barricaded to keep people safe till we could secure the town or at least this section of it gemma helped clear out the buildings and helped teach people how to secure in an emergency she had an idea about building underground escape routs but I figured that would come at a later date as at the moment the more pressing issue was the zombies themselves it was harder than I thought not as much the zombies being clumped together it was that the houses seemed to just be hidden around cornors or in the rooms it was a nightmare the children zombies started to appear more we killed as quickly and as quietly the problem was that the zombies didn't even seem agitated when they were killed like before it was almost Asif they wanted them to fall so another could rise up the first block of houses was cleared quickly a few people came out and tried to settle in im not going to lie I would want to stay in the safety of the walls but maybe if they hide in plane site that zombies won't be all over them as quickly the children from our survivors were playing by the time I returned to the compound they all seemed completely unaware of the danger they were in I asked Sarah if I could have a chat about something very personal she responded that yes she would come and have a word with me shortly after she kept her word and arrived at the right moment I was full of fear not because of the zombies but because their lack of careing I asked if she had seen anything about this kind of thing she replied that maybe the zombie leader of this area was dead and that they had no cause I dismissed this as they still attacked even attacking at the fourths I mentioned another reason I pulled her to one side I realized that once the area was secure the fourths would be working their way to fight other zombie leaders around the country and eventually the world and id have to go with them as their leader she got the idea of what I was talking about but didn't want to discuss it until the time was right I mentioned that there was never going to be a time that was right I needed to know that she would keep my family and friends safe once I left as the chances where that I would not be returning even after the war on the undead was won if it ever was won she asked me what she needed to do I gave her a list and told her these preparations needed making I knew this was going to be a one way trip anyway I went back out to try clear out the rest of the area in Stockwell it took so long it felt like days I got a call from the short range radio asking for me to go back that I was needed on my way through one of the houses that I had cleared I fell through the floor to what seemed like a tunnel that had been dug Knaresborough is well known for having lots of secret tunnels but this looked fresh and I could smell the stench of death and decay I tried to call on the radio but the signal seemed to be jammed I cursed as I couldn't fly yet I tried my hardest but failed I figured I may as well follow it to my horror the direction in which it was headed was underneath the FOB I started to panic thinking was someone trying to get to us under cover of night or was it something more sinister as I got deeper and deeper I found bodies half decayed but these where a lot older than 6 days they looked years older and the tunnels looked brand new I panic and pick up the pace till I could hear soldiers above me I punched the ground it collapsed above my head low and behold I was right under where I had been staying thinking as fast as I could I ordered the tunnel be collapsed and a survey of the area be taken as this tunnel had been dug recently by either the living or the dead I decided to go back down the tunnel with the fourths and follow it right the other way past where I had fallen through the floor as it carried on the smell got worse and worse the further we went it felt like we had walked for hours and hours when reality was that we had walked for ten minutes I figured we must be right under the castle at this stage and that meant that the tunnel would turn into the castle but instead it went deeper into the ground it started spiraling now I could hear a growl of what I could only assume was zombies a horde maybe large maybe small but their was that oh so familiar sound the where headed straight for us and their was no way out only thing left to do was to stand and fight them so we lined up grabbed our swords from our sides armoured up and got ready what presented us was not hundreds of zombies but a whole legion of them I new that this time may be our last stand against the zombies and so to make things better I pulled out my phone started playing music to fight to that's when he appeared ADAM I thought you where dead I exclaim nope he replied mearly wounded when the zombie overlord found me he revived me learnt everything he could about you and made it his soul purpose to kill you I have been told to offer you a choice surrender you and your fourths and the rest of the humans in this zone or be destroyed I respond without warning all the other fourths follow my rallying battle cry adam replies with a simple I was hoeping as much my dear zombies would you be so kind as to bring me their heads on spikes with that he darted to the back of the horde they started running straight at us we plowed through them almost asif a symbiotic link had been made we predicted each others moves and supported each other in a matter of moments we have slain over a hundred zombies that's when I saw Gabriel join the fight only he wasn't fighting the zombies he was fighting with Kyle he wasn't even paying attention to the zombies that's when I noticed he had a bite mark on his neck yet he still seemed to have control of his armor it carried on even though its wielder was clearly undead he tore through Kyles armor and ripped out Kyles heart killing him instantly at least it was a clean death i ran at Gabriel while the others surrounded us and made sure no zombies could get involved I looked at Gabriel and asked why he chose to turn his back on humanity he simply responded with immortality is the price offered to turn my back on humanity I couldn't stand it I needed to get past him and deal with Adam but he refused to let me past him Kyles body started to get back up but one of the fourths was on it already the armor fell apart in his hands Kyle was put to rest permanently moments later I grab onto Gabriel and smash my foot into his chest harder than any human possibly could it winded him but clearly wasn't going to go down without a fight he drew his now mutated sword I wasn't ready for a sword fight but I drew mine anyway he swung for me with all he had his sword seemed slower and he didn't seem to be able to sink up to us as we all were connected he had disconnected from our formation so I was able to side step his sword and smash him in the face with my fist it knocked a tooth out but nothing more than that he was bleeding but not normal blood it was thicker I guess this is what the zombies had in them too but no time to look and wait he swings for me one more time before I decide enough is enough I drop kick him he hits the deck and hard I land on top of him and remember what he said only way to kill a zombie overlord is to take the head off then WP them I slices his head off and ram the WP down his neck his body blows up we still all feel pain and betrayal of his disloyal actions as his body finally was destroyed the other fourths made a formation around me telling me I needed to deal with Adam and that they would hold off the zombies as long as they could I ran in the direction Adam had just left in I found him surrounded by zombie dogs and the big fuckers so I laugh and say is this all you have a small army I am a one man army and I'll take you all unshaken the undead look to their master to get permission Adam waves his hand and the massacre begins I put down all of the minions of his and make sure none of them are getting back up when it is finally just me and him he looks more afraid than I've ever seen him he looked like he was about to try bargain for his life and try to blame someone else say he was forced to do it I silence him I pick him up and smash his body into the ground hard his skull cracks open but it doesn't kill him I don't want him to die to quickly especially after what he did to my sister I want this mother fucker to pay for what he's done he realizes he is going to die and just sits on the ground and waits he looks at me and says well go on then get on with it there is no sport killing a zombie when it wants to die it's a play he makes he thinks he's caught me off guard when the end of the barrel on my gun is right inside his skull he says fuuuuuuuuuuccccckkkk and I pull the trigger his brains splatter every corner of the room that's when I see the zombie overlord he comes down from the ceiling and asks if he may approach me I except his offer no point in not being civil about this he comes down lands about twenty feet away from me he says I'm going to make you an offer if you refuse you will die if you except you will die as a matter of principle but will be brought back I want you to lead my army like Adam did but better I want you to show me what It means to be a fourth I look at him in disbelief how dare you offer me that role I would rather take death than take you up on that shit offer so be it said the zombie overlord he ran at me but this time I wasn't alone with him the other fourths appeared out of what felt like thin air together smashing and cutting into him making this into our own personal vendetta against this dick he tried to offer us immortality to give up on humanity and take up beside him and serve with him however tempting this may be we can never give in to offers like that we must stand together as one Beth said at that moment the zombie lord slices open her neck she bleeds to death but she won't be coming back he made sure of that it's me and a few other fourths left now the two silent ones start working their way into him kicking him slicing him and making him work to try and wound one of us it's not possible we get the better of him he collapses on the floor in a heap like the lord before him we cut his head off and WP him to oblivion that is when I realize this is where the lords are coming from we could destroy the lord of the area permanently if we blew this bit to kingdom come I remembered that there was people up above unaware of what danger they are in I grab the other fourths assemble them it may be awhile before an opportunity to permanently end the zombie lord in this area arises again if we do this we may end up losing our lives they agree that this is what their purpose is and always has been to serve the human race and give back to them at their time of need we place explosives at the base of the egg where the lords where spawning I tell all the others to leave and to get as far away from the blast as possible to serve my life would be an honor to save what remained of the humanity that resided above where I currently stood they stand by my side and refuse to leave even after they have been ordered to leave they refused I plant the last charge and I pull the trigger I see a bright light but then I see my feet are in the air and that the others are carrying me out with flight we are racing the flames I wish there was something I could do I watched the zombies underneath me burn to a wither and to toast I smile as I no they can no longer hurt anyone we hit the surface the building above us catches fire we fly out and then land on the road all the zombies around us are perfectly still almost motionless I walk up to one literally right in its face still nothing I cut its head off none of the zombies react they are all immobile I see the children zombies all dead on the floor the big fuckers have even stopped I realized what had happened because we had killed the zombie overlord they had no function and would be unable to move without leadership so they were slowly dying as we walked down the street the zombies had all stopped every were within Knaresborough they had all come to a complete stand still it was so beautiful to see soldiers were doing clean up killing them and burning them with no resistance when I finally found Gemma she was crying at the fact that Knaresborough was finally safe again the fourths were celebrated but the cleanup was far from over the zombies still needed to be killed and burnt to stop them from ever returning to the living to feed once the clean up was done I set the builders the biggest task of their lives setting up a massive wall around Knaresborough to protect it and to turn it into a sanctuary for all living people and animals I made sure the what soliders where left were to protect the area at all cost they humbaly agreed the next thing to happen was possibly the hardest thing I had ever done I had to say goodbye to Gemma as the fight for the country still had to continue we had secured one area but the world still needed the fourths when Gemma finally asked me will I see you again I replied with all the love in my heart that as long as there was breath in my body then I would come back to her at the end of this shit storm there was a celebration in the name of the fourths that would be remembered in history as the day the zombies lost north Yorkshire we danced we celebrated but mainly we mourned our fallen brothers and sisters some we knew others where not known I finally let out my emotions about all the family I had lost Gemma knew I was struggling and so she hugged up to me the best feeling in the world is knowing that the ones you love are safe I remember saying to her she cried so much that it made me cry at that point nearly half the town was crying where would I head she asked I remembered that the rest of the country and the world needed to be recovered from these undead scum however I wouldn't stop even if it killed me I was still unsure what had caused this deadly outbreak but was about to find out on my long and weary travels...............

Lightning Source UK Ltd.
Milton Keynes UK
UKHW020644171022
410608UK00017B/947